The MACAT Library
世界思想宝库钥匙丛书

解析W.E.B.杜波依斯

《黑人的灵魂》

AN ANALYSIS OF

W. E. B. DU BOIS'S

THE SOULS OF BLACK FOLK

Jason Xidias ◎ 著

王作伟 ◎ 译

上海外语教育出版社
外教社 SHANGHAI FOREIGN LANGUAGE EDUCATION PRESS

目　录

CONTENTS

引言

要 点

- W. E. B. 杜波依斯（1868—1963）的教学、研究、新闻报道和行动，催生了终结美国种族隔离和亚非殖民主义的运动。
- 《黑人的灵魂》认为白人编造了种族主义的概念以促进他们的物质财富积累。这对黑人的身份、民主和人性产生了严重的负面影响，只有黑人的骄傲、反抗和斗争才能将其克服。
- 《黑人的灵魂》反对 20 世纪早期美国的"黑人在生理上不如白人"的主流观点，这样的观点也解释了黑人社会地位的问题。

W. E. B. 杜波依斯其人

W. E. B. 杜波依斯 1868 年生于马萨诸塞州的大巴灵顿，是一位出色的学者。1895 年，他成为第一位获得哈佛大学博士学位的非裔美国人。后来，他以教授、记者和活动家的身份，为社会做出了巨大贡献。他一生都致力于揭露美国和其他地方种族主义的真正原因，阐释了种族主义对黑人身份的影响。他主张必须克服种族主义，以实现真正的民主和对人类更为深刻和全面的理解。弗雷德里克·道格拉斯 * 摆脱了奴隶制，成为了一位杰出的黑人知识分子。杜波依斯继承并发扬了他的伟大遗产，成为结束美国种族隔离和亚非殖民主义运动的核心力量，因此被认为是历史上最伟大的人物之一。

《黑人的灵魂》的主要内容

杜波依斯于 1903 年出版了《黑人的灵魂》。该书基于作者的个人经历和研究，由 14 篇关于种族主义的文章组成，其中一些已经在文学与文化杂志《大西洋月刊》* 上发表。

在《黑人的灵魂》中，杜波依斯使用一系列的文学技巧来描述吉姆·克劳法时期＊美国社会中的种族主义和不平等状况。这个漫长的时期始于1877年，于20世纪60年代结束。当时，各州政府实施了各种助长种族主义、种族隔离和不平等的措施，而这些措施随后得到了国家联邦立法的支持。尽管1865年美国宪法＊第十三修正案废除了奴隶制，1870年通过的第十五修正案赋予了黑人选举权，但是这些还是发生了。

《黑人的灵魂》挑战了认为"黑人在生理上和文化上都不如白人"的主流学术观点。英国博物学家＊查尔斯·达尔文＊是提出这一观点的人之一。杜波依斯反对这一观点，详尽地揭示了白人如何通过编造"种族主义"概念来累积他们的物质财富。

在《黑人的灵魂》一书中，杜波依斯认为，他对种族主义的隐喻"肤色界线"目前和将来都是美国20世纪面临的最大问题。在他看来，种族主义破坏了民主和人性。若要让美国真正成为一贯宣称的"上帝庇佑下不可分割的国家"，那么白人必须承认过去，黑人必须是平等的公民。杜波依斯引用了德国哲学家格 G. W. F. 黑格尔＊1807年的著作《精神现象学》中对历史和意识＊（即自我意识）的分析，认为种族主义妨碍了美国白人和黑人发挥他们的潜能。

如他之前的弗雷德里克·道格拉斯一样，杜波依斯鼓励黑人接受教育，成为领袖，以自己的传统和文化而自豪，敢于同白人的压迫作斗争。这一立场与当时另一位伟大的非裔美国人布克·T. 华盛顿＊的观点形成了鲜明的对比。华盛顿认为，黑人应该适应白人倡导的种族主义，以换取基本的教育和法律权利。

在《黑人的灵魂》中，杜波依斯引入了两个重要的概念，进一步发展了他对"肤色界线"的观点。第一个是"双重意识"，指在白人种族主义社会中，黑人想同时成为非洲人和美国人所面临的重重困难。第二个是"面纱"，喻指种族主义是一种划分黑人和白人的边界，这对黑人和白人的灵魂都是沉重的负担，阻碍他们充分发挥自己的潜能。

在整部书中，杜波依斯明确表示，他乐观地认为有一天美国将揭开这一"面纱"。他相信，当白人承认过去的不公正，并且黑人成为平等的公民时，这一愿景就能实现。那时，美国将成为一个真正的民主国家，人道将超越一切，美国的灵魂才会平和安宁。

《黑人的灵魂》的学术价值

在《黑人的灵魂》中，杜波依斯反对美国 20 世纪早期的"黑人在生理上不如白人"的观点，同时提出了替代布克·T. 华盛顿妥协立场的另一种选择。杜波依斯提出资本主义*经济体制导致白人种族主义，并鼓励黑人进行斗争，从而确立了书中论点。这本书使人们深入了解了种族歧视的成因、它对身份的影响以及如何战胜它。虽然《黑人的灵魂》重点刻画的是吉姆·克劳时期的美国社会，但他后来的作品在全球层面上触及了种族主义问题，有力地支持了所有被压迫少数族裔的集体抗争。以《黑人的灵魂》为代表，杜波依斯的作品鼓舞了世界各地的活动家。《黑人的灵魂》融汇了非裔美国人研究、种族与民族理论批判和后殖民主义研究。作为从历史学到社会学、从经济学到政治学等许多领域进一步研究的起点，这本书具有巨大的跨学科价值。

第一部分：学术渊源

1 作者生平与历史背景

要点 🔑

- 《黑人的灵魂》是社会学重要著作、美国文学经典，是美国历史上关于种族主义和黑人身份的最重要的文献之一。

- 1885 年，杜波依斯从北部的马萨诸塞州搬到南方的田纳西州学习，对美国的种族主义有了更深的了解。

- 吉姆·克劳时代，州政府和地方政府公然立法歧视黑人。该时代始于 1877 年，一直持续到 20 世纪 60 年代的民权运动。

为何要读这部著作？

《黑人的灵魂》是由美国历史学家、社会学家和民权活动家 W. E. B. 杜波依斯撰写的 14 篇关于种族主义的文章的合集。该书出版于 1903 年，是美国社会学领域最重要的文献之一，也是美国文学的经典之作。想要了解构成美国黑人历史的诸多要素，就必须阅读《黑人的灵魂》。这些要素包括：

- 黑人的身份和其对身份的认识（意识）
- 黑人经历的歧视与不平等
- 种族主义与经济学之间的联系
- 教育和领导能力在改变中的作用
- 消除不公正以达到更高层次人性的需要

杜波依斯在其著作中（使用多种不同的方法）把社会分析、宗教信仰、文学隐喻和科学研究结合在了一起。因此，他得以对 19 世纪末 20 世纪初美国种族主义以及黑人的抗争进行了全面而深入的分析。在《黑人的灵魂》中，作者表达了一种悲哀，但同时也有一种深深的乐观。杜波依斯相信，总有一天，黑人的反抗和斗争会战胜吉姆·克劳法（这些法律使种族隔离在州和地方层面合法化，造成了对黑人的压迫和不平等现象）。正如他在书中预言的那样："有一天，觉醒将至，那时千万灵魂被压抑的生命力将势不可挡地冲向目标，冲出死亡笼罩的幽谷*。"1

杜波依斯的核心思想贯穿全书。他认为种族主义是一种利用种族、阶级和性别来实现政治和经济目的的社会建构。其目的是对黑人进行分类、羞辱和剥削，主要是为了赚钱。他说，这可以从他所处社会当下的现实和美国奴隶制的历史中看到。作者认为，只有黑人的骄傲、反抗和斗争的"大觉醒"才能战胜种族主义。在现实生活中，这意味着黑人不仅拥有平等的合法公民身份和投票权，而且在教育和就业方面也有与白人同等的机会。只有如此，无论白人黑人，大家才能摆脱过去的苦难，享有更广泛的人性权利。

> "历史不能忽视 W. E. B. 杜波依斯，因为历史必须反映真理。杜波依斯博士是一位对社会真理孜孜不倦的探索者和天赋异禀的发现者。他的伟大之处在于对自己民族的真理的不懈寻求。很少有学者对黑人进行切实的研究，而他试图填补这一巨大的空白。他所取得的成就揭示了人类的巨大维度。"
>
> ——马丁·路德·金*博士

作者生平

W. E. B. 杜波依斯于 1868 年生于马萨诸塞州的大巴灵顿。他的母亲有非洲、英国与荷兰的血统。正因如此，杜波依斯属于马萨诸塞州一个拥有自由和土地的黑人小群体。他的母亲玛丽是一名佣人，父亲阿尔弗雷德失业，所以家境十分拮据。威廉出生一年后，父亲阿尔弗雷德便离弃了这个家庭，再也没有回来。母亲玛丽在威廉17岁时去世，从此，他成了一个可怜的孤儿。

杜波依斯就读于一所白人为主的学校，并在一所白人新教徒*为主的教堂做礼拜。他天资聪颖，1884年成为所在高中第一个黑人毕业生，获得了很高的荣誉。靠着工作攒下的积蓄和当地教会的资助，杜波依斯上了位于田纳西州纳什维尔的菲斯克大学并且获得了文学学士学位。后来，又在家乡马萨诸塞州的哈佛大学获得历史学学位。在吉姆·克劳法被完全接受的美国南部菲斯克的经历，彻底改变了杜波依斯对社会的看法。正是在那里，杜波依斯深入了解了美国的种族主义及其对黑人身份的影响。[2]

杜波依斯在哈佛从未有过归属感，但他深知在美国最受尊敬的大学里学习，对他的智力发展和声誉是多么重要。他一直强调，良好的教育是黑人改变社会地位和反抗压迫的主要途径。杜波依斯成为哈佛大学第一位非裔美国人博士研究生。他的博士学位论文写于历史系，题目是《对美利坚合众国的非洲奴隶贸易的平抑过程（1638—1870）》。同时，他还在柏林的弗里德里希威廉大学学习过，研究了社会学家和哲学家马克斯·韦伯*、卡尔·马克思*和其他主要德国学者的著作。[3]大概在这个时期，在社会主义思想的影响下，[4]杜波依斯第一次写下了他"为黑人的崛起而奋斗"的愿望。[5]他终其余生，通过学术研究和教学（在威尔伯福斯大学、宾夕法尼亚大学和亚特兰大大学）以及他的新闻报道与政治活动来促进平等。

创作背景

1903 年，在吉姆·克劳法的背景下，杜波依斯出版了他最重要的著作《黑人的灵魂》。1870 年，美国国会*通过了宪法第 15 条修正案，赋予非裔美国人选举权。然而，从 1877 年重建*结束——1861—65 年美国内战*之后的国家重建——直到 20 世纪 60 年代的民权运动，南方白人采取了大量措施来阻碍黑人实现平等。例如，从 1890 年到 1910 年，新颁布的州宪法和法律强加了税收和读写能力测验*，这些都是精心策划以阻止黑人投票的，尽管黑人有合法的投票权。税收突然成为选举注册条件之一，任何人如果不能纳税或不能阅读，就不允许投票。此外，白人对黑人的恐吓也阻碍了实现平等的进程。

与此同时，1896 年最高法院的普莱西诉弗格森案*确立，联邦政府不能干预阻止各州在就业、住房和公共交通等重要领域实施地方种族隔离法。[6]

1885 年，杜波依斯决定离开马萨诸塞州前往田纳西州的菲斯克大学时，他知道他将对美国的种族主义有更深的了解。他写道，"我要去南方，有奴隶制、叛乱和黑人的南方；最重要的是，我将遇到同我年龄和教育程度相仿、和我有同样抱负的有色人种。"[7]

在菲斯克大学，杜波依斯很快注意到，因为在内战中失败，未能脱离现有的联邦以及 1865 年奴隶制的废除，南方白人心怀怨恨。此外，他还目睹了黑人遭受的极端贫困、机会短缺和暴力。就像他说的，"只有未曾有过任何肤色种姓经历就去了南方的黑人，才能理解这种野蛮。我只感觉到轻蔑和憎恨；是那种狗可能会招致的轻蔑……谋杀、杀害和伤害黑人，强奸黑人妇女……这甚至算不上新闻，没有曝光，也没有人被逮捕。"[8]

正是吉姆·克劳法时期种族歧视的历史背景和杜波依斯在美国北部和南部以及欧洲的亲身经历，推动他成为美国黑人事业以及世界各地黑人的领袖。杜波依斯对正义的热情从 19 世纪的最后十年一直持续到 1963 年。那一年，他在新独立的加纳去世，享年 95 岁。

---

1. W. E. B. 杜波依斯：《黑人的灵魂》，纽约、伦敦：W. W. 诺顿公司，1999 年，第 xxxi 页。

2. 杜波依斯：《黑人的灵魂》，第 xiii—xv 页。

3. 杜波依斯：《黑人的灵魂》，第 xvi—xix 页。

4. 张聚国：《杜波依斯与美国种族问题》，纽约：劳特利奇出版社，2001 年，第 135 页。

5. 杜波依斯：《黑人的灵魂》，第 xvii、xviii 页。

6. 约瑟夫·摩根·寇瑟：《1880—1910 年间南方政治的塑造：选举权的限制与南方一党制的建立》，纽黑文：耶鲁大学出版社，1974 年。

7. 杜波依斯：《黑人的灵魂》，1999 年，第 xxv 页。

8. 杜波依斯：《黑人的灵魂》，1999 年，第 xxv 页。

2 学术背景

要点 🗝

- 杜波依斯认为，白人从社会层面上构建了或者编造了"种族"的概念来牟利。这一观点是对"黑人在生理和文化上都不如白人"主流观点的挑战。

- 杜波依斯的灵感来自弗雷德里克·道格拉斯的斗争。道格拉斯在19世纪摆脱奴役，成为著名的黑人知识分子领袖。

- 杜波依斯把德国哲学家 G. W. F. 黑格尔对历史与意识之间关系的理解应用到对美国种族主义和非裔美国人的分裂意识的研究上。

著作语境

社会学，即社会行为的科学研究，是一个相对现代的概念，起源于 18 世纪晚期。该学科的发展是科学进步、宗教影响力下降、工业化和城市化（人口从农村向城市转移）的结果。

1903 年，杜波依斯出版《黑人的灵魂》时，大多数社会学家认为人类的进步是随着我们人类在生物层面的进化而发生的。19世纪中叶的英国早期社会学家赫伯特·斯宾塞 * 即是这种观点的拥护者。他的观点与曾出版过《物种起源》*（1859）和《人类的起源》（1871）的英国著名博物学家查尔斯·达尔文的观点密切相关。达尔文认为，"白人和黑人种族"在智力水平上不同。[1]

这些思想是在 18 世纪晚期的启蒙运动 * 中发展起来的，启蒙运动从人类的理性和科学中寻找答案。在美国，支持进化生物学 * 的观点与斯宾塞强调黑人的"停滞发展"和"原始本性"如出一辙。欧洲殖民列强通过传播自身天生就比原住民优越的观点，来为他们在非洲和亚洲的扩张和剥削进行辩护。事实上，他们认为引导亚非人走向"更高级的存在状态"是他们的职责。这一观点有时被称为"白人的负担"，[2] 取自英国作家拉迪亚德·吉卜林 * 的同名诗歌。这种领土扩张也被称为教化使命 *。

美国内战结束后，美国经历了快速的工业化和城市化进程，大量的人口涌向城市寻找工作，其中许多人是黑人。学者们开始运用科学方法 * 来研究美国的社会状况。这种方法包括提出一个问题和预测可能的答案，然后进行测试和实验来证明这个答案的对错。几所大学开始设置社会学博士课程。1895 年，W. E. B. 杜波依斯成为第一个获得哈佛大学博士学位的非裔美国人。

《黑人的灵魂》挑战了白人生而优越的主流观念，为社会学领域做出了开创性的贡献。该书认为，美国的白人精英刻意创造了一个种族主义盛行的社会，不平等是资本主义和美国黑人奴隶制历史的直接结果。这两个因素使得黑人很难取得进步。

> "白人的幸福不能用黑人的痛苦来换取，白人的美德不能通过黑人的堕落来达到……很明显，白人和黑人必须'兴衰相伴，同舟共济'。"
>
> —— 弗雷德里克·道格拉斯，《弗雷德里克·道格拉斯：演讲和写作精选》

学科概览

法国哲学家奥古斯特·孔德 * 被公认为社会学的奠基人，[3] 他的著作《实证主义总论》（1848）首次提出了利用自然科学的科学方法来研究社会结构的思想。

12

孔德受到理性的、基于科学的启蒙运动思想的启发，认为社会进化包括三个阶段。第一个是神学阶段，主张宗教决定一个人在社会中的地位。换句话说，每个人在社会阶梯上都有"上帝赋予"的位置。例如，国王就在阶梯的顶端，因为他声称自己与上帝有着独特的关系。

第二阶段是形而上学阶段，即理性的科学思想通过促进对普世权利和人类进步的尊重来挑战"上帝赋予"的阶段。1789 年的法国大革命*和《人权宣言》*就是这样的例子。

最后一个阶段是实证主义阶段，即积极运用科学的方法研究不平等之类的问题，而不仅仅是接受《人权宣言》等作品中提出的自然权利和平等的理念。

像孔德一样，德国革命社会主义者卡尔·马克思也运用科学的方法来理解社会的变化和进步。自 19 世纪 40 年代开始，他就认为历史是统治阶级和工人阶级斗争的产物。他相信工人们最终会团结起来推翻统治阶级和资本主义本身，用一个没有剥削的共产主义*社会取而代之。马克思的观点和杜波依斯的观点有明显的相似之处，杜波依斯认为美国的种族主义是建立在经济学基础之上的。值得注意的是，在杜波依斯写《黑人的灵魂》的时候，马克思在美国学术界的影响还是很有限的。[4]

学术渊源

美国作家拉尔夫·沃尔多·爱默生*在他 1843 年的著作《超验论者》中创造了"双重意识"这个术语。杜波依斯将这个概念扩展到"种族关系"的社会心理学中。他用这个术语来解释这种心理状态：既有非洲血统，又有奴隶制下欧洲或美国的"教养"。杜波依斯把这种双重意识描述为"通过别人的眼睛审视自己的生命"。

在哈佛，杜波依斯研究了德国哲学。在写《黑人的灵魂》时，他借鉴了 G. W. F. 黑格尔的《精神现象学》。文学教授沙蒙·查米尔*认为，黑格尔为杜波依斯提供了把"意识与历史的关系"理论化的方法。[5]

在现象学中，黑格尔用了主人和奴隶的例子来说明不平等的权力关系是怎样导致个体不被认同的。这反过来会导致一个人自我意识（即作为一个人对自身的认识）的缺失。为了获得自由和实现自我（能够实现自己的潜能），必须要让别人认同自己是一个自主的（自治的）个体。如果没有这样的认同，主人就定义了奴隶的身份，而奴隶作为个体的自我意识就遭到破坏，从而导致奴隶处于被压迫的状态。

杜波依斯将黑格尔的概念应用于"解放后的美国"（奴隶制废除后的时期），认为白人种族主义对黑人的身份有着严重的影响。在 1865 年内战结束后的重建时期，非裔美国人取得了很重要的成就，其中包括废除*奴隶制、禁止种族歧视、取得公民身份和选举权。尽管如此，杜波依斯展示了在奴隶制度下存在的权力关系是如何被吉姆·克劳法复制的，这些法律在所谓的"分裂但平等"的社会中促使了歧视的产生。这导致了另一种形式的再次奴役，各州禁止种族间通婚，在种族间实行种族隔离，专门制定了读写测验和人头税*以防止黑人投票。

杜波依斯认为，这种再次奴役在非裔美国人心中产生了一种分裂意识，唯有通过社会冲突和白人对平等的最终认可才能消除。

最后，苏格兰哲学家托马斯·卡莱尔*的作品激发了杜波依斯想要成为黑人事业领袖的愿望。[6]卡莱尔提出了伟人理论*，认为伟人通过利用他们的天分、智慧、魅力和政治敏锐性来创造历史。从这个角度来说，杜波依斯希望能继承弗雷德里克·道格拉斯的事业。道格拉斯曾是一个逃亡的奴隶，但通过卓越的学识最终成长为领导黑人进行抵抗和斗争的领袖。

---

1. 查尔斯·达尔文：《人类的起源》，伦敦：约翰·莫蕾出版社，1871 年，第 216—217 页。

2. 拉迪亚德·吉卜林："白人的负担"，《麦克卢尔杂志》，1899 年第 12 期，第 290—291 页。

3. 例如，见奥古斯特·孔德：《孔德早期的政治著作选》封底，H. S. 琼斯编，剑桥：剑桥大学出版社，1998 年。

4. 长期以来一直存在争论：为什么美国从未有过与一些欧洲国家类似的社会主义影响／劳工运动？这可以追溯到亚历西斯·德·托克维尔"美国例外论"的观点。例如，西摩·马丁·利普塞特和加里·马克思：《未生此地：为什么社会主义在美国失败了》，纽约：W. W. 诺顿出版公司，2001 年。

5. 沙蒙·扎米尔：《W. E. B. 杜波依斯和美国思想：1888—1903》，芝加哥：芝加哥大学，1995 年，第 117 页。

6. 更多细节，见张聚国：《W. E. B. 杜波依斯与美国种族问题》，纽约：劳特利奇出版社，2001 年，W. E. B.，第 29 页。

3 主导命题

要点 ⚷

- 《黑人的灵魂》出版时，黑人知识分子的一个主要问题是：在种族主义的美国，非裔美国人如何才能最好地提升他们的社会地位？

- 1895 年，当时的杰出黑人知识分子布克·T.华盛顿同意南方白人的观点，即黑人应接受白人的政治统治，以换取基本的教育和法律权利，这就是所谓的亚特兰大妥协案 *。

- 杜波依斯认为，黑人不应该妥协，应该与白人种族主义斗争以实现平等。

核心问题

《黑人的灵魂》探讨了三个核心问题：

- 为什么在内战和重建之后，白人仍继续压迫非裔美国人？
- 种族主义如何影响非裔美国人的身份？
- 非裔美国人如何在种族主义社会中提升社会地位？

W. E. B. 杜波依斯带着悲伤、痛苦和希望回应了这些问题。

对于杜波依斯来说，弗雷德里克·道格拉斯是"美国最伟大的黑人领袖"。[1] 道格拉斯摆脱了奴役，成为社会改革家、公共演说家和有影响力的作家。他领导了废奴运动 * 来结束奴隶制，并在亚伯拉罕·林肯 * 总统 1863 年起草《解放奴隶宣言》* 中发挥了关键作用。宣言指出，在反叛的南方各州，所有的奴隶都将获得自由。道格拉斯一生写了三部自传，当中描述了美国根深蒂固的种族主义，并呼吁黑人进行斗争。

杜波依斯深受道格拉斯之死的影响，他在一系列名为《道格拉斯的逝世》的哀歌*中表达了内心深处的情感。杜波依斯想通过成为非裔美国人事业的新领袖来继承和发扬道格拉斯的精神。他始终秉持"种族主义是一种剥削黑人劳动的政治经济工具"的观点，成功地延续了道格拉斯的工作。

> "华盛顿先生的错误和缺点是确定无疑的：他从未充分把握政治和工业之间日益紧密的联系……黑人民权丧失、黑人大学和公立学校减少以及在这片土地上出现更加固化的种族等级制。为了庄严的正义，我们必须让华盛顿先生的灵魂担负终结这一切的重大责任。"
>
> —— 杜波依斯：《黑人的灵魂》

参与者

1845 年，弗雷德里克·道格拉斯出版了他的第一部自传《弗雷德里克·道格拉斯：一个美国奴隶的生平自述》。这本书追溯了作者的生平以及逃离奴役的过程，集中讲述了奴隶主对奴隶的残酷统治，以及他自己工作到筋疲力尽、无法干活时被鞭打的经历。这本书在美国 19 世纪中期的废奴运动中发挥了重要作用，初版时就售出了成千上万册，[2] 挑战了白人的"黑人不聪明，没有能力从事智力工作"的主流观点。道格拉斯接着又出版了两本自传，《我的奴隶生涯和我的自由》（1855）以及《弗雷德里克·道格拉斯的生平和时代》（1881）。

杜波依斯认为道格拉斯是最伟大的黑人榜样。他担心，在道格拉斯死后，布克·T. 华盛顿会成为非裔美国人群体的主导人物。杜波依斯并不认为华盛顿代表了集体的利益。1895 年，华盛顿批评黑人在重建过程中寻求政治和经济权力，并与南方白人达成了一项协议，即"亚特兰大妥协案"。该协议宣布，南方黑人将服从白人的政治统治，以换取基本的教育和法律权利。

当时的论战

华盛顿认为，黑人应该原谅过去的不公正，接受歧视，接受旨在促进就业的工业技术教育，融入主流社会，通过努力工作和消费产品向白人证明，他们可以得到更好的待遇。根据亚特兰大妥协案，黑人不会起来反对种族主义，也不会要求选举权。

杜波依斯强烈反对华盛顿的立场，声称如果黑人接受了这种关系，他们只会延续白人的压迫。杜波依斯提出的另一种建议是，黑人应该抵制所有的统治，为公民平等、选举权、教育平等和建立一个真正的精英体制而奋斗，在这个体制中，个体的能力，而非种族，才是评判的标准。

《黑人的灵魂》为发展中的黑人集体意识（作为一个群体的意识）和黑人集体文化发声。当时，过去的奴隶和奴隶的后代正在努力了解自己是谁，以及在内战和重建的余波后，他们的集体代表了什么。杜波依斯领导了黑人反抗白人统治，在奴隶制的混乱中指引黑人进行了斗争。他还激起了黑人对吉姆·克劳法的反抗，那时的法律明显地倾向于通过种族隔离以及从黑人教育机构撤回援助，使非裔美国人在民权上处于劣势。

由于上述原因，《黑人的灵魂》是对白人的主导地位和布克·T. 华盛顿立场的非常重要的回应。华盛顿倾向于在亚特兰大妥协案体制内来努力改善黑人的境况。而该书则为美国种族主义提供了另一种观点，并提供了应对策略。它也为实现黑人进步和发展黑人中产阶级的途径提供了理论支持。

1. 杜波依斯：《黑人的灵魂》，第 xxi 页。

2. 弗雷德里克·道格拉斯：《弗雷德里克·道格拉斯：一个美国奴隶的生平自述》引言，本杰明·夸尔斯编，马萨诸塞州剑桥：哈佛大学出版社，1988 年。

4 作者贡献

要点

- 《黑人的灵魂》中所蕴含的思想继承和发扬了曾是奴隶和黑人知识分子的弗雷德里克·道格拉斯的思想，为美国和其他地方的黑人提供了灵感。他们反对布克·T.华盛顿的妥协立场。
- 这本书质疑了学术界和政界认为"黑人在生理和文化上都不如白人"的主流观点。
- 杜波依斯认为，在他的国家，种族主义是一个被编造出来的概念，扎根于资本主义和美国奴隶制的遗留问题之中。他相信黑人的反抗、骄傲和斗争最终会战胜偏见。

作者目标

W. E. B.杜波依斯的《黑人的灵魂》使曾是奴隶的弗雷德里克·道格拉斯的思想遗产得以复兴，并使其重回美国政治议程。道格拉斯曾领导过美国废奴运动，在黑人中声名鹊起，是一位有魅力、有说服力的作家和演说家。他为普世平等而战，敢于质疑白人认为"黑人不够聪明以至于不能成为知识分子"的主流观念。他的自传描绘了亲历的奴隶制的恐怖，但他的成功脱逃和功成名就也使许多人受到鼓舞。

1895年道格拉斯死后，布克·T.华盛顿成为美国最受认可的黑人知识分子之一。他认为，黑人应该在短期内服从种族主义和白人的政治统治，以换取基本的权利。通过学术研究、新闻报道和社会活动，杜波依斯挑战了"黑人在生理上比白人低劣"的观点，揭露了白人资本主义的贪婪是如何通过奴隶制和种族主义从廉价劳动力中牟利的。这一立场在当时是革命性的，并引发了各种各样的反应。[1] 与华盛顿认为黑人应该接受"二等公民"身份的观点不同，杜波依斯认为，白人和黑人可以克服过去的不公正，并且建立一个以平等为基础的人道社会。

> "杜波依斯博士不仅是一位探索知识前沿的巨人，首先，他是一名教师。……他在教学中坚持的一个观点是，黑人被一种恶毒的谎言所压迫和剥削。这些谎言把他们描述为低人一等，天生有缺陷，注定要被奴役至坟墓的人。……这种歪曲的逻辑认为，如果黑人是劣等的，他就没有受到压迫——他在社会中的地位与他贫乏的才能和才智是相称的。"
>
> —— 马丁·路德·金博士

研究方法

与社会学和社会科学的发展相一致，杜波依斯运用科学方法（通过实验和实实在在的数据来寻求问题的答案）来理解社会问题——如种族主义和不平等——以及它们对非裔美国人身份的影响。

1903 年出版的《黑人的灵魂》是以杜波依斯四年前出版的另一开创性著作《费城黑人》为基础的。后者是社会学作为统计科学的最早的例子之一，结合了 5 000 多篇对普通人的采访和人口普查数据，[2] 生动地描绘了居住在宾夕法尼亚州费城的非裔美国人在社会和经济方面遭受剥夺的状况。

《黑人的灵魂》开拓了人们的视野，因为它直面"经过科学证明"的所谓"低劣的生物特性使黑人无法实现平等"的立场。杜波依斯解释了白人是如何建构一个他们在智力上和道德上都被认为很优越的社会，他们利用"种族差异"的概念来剥削黑人来为自己赚钱。因此，他认为白人反被禁锢在自我否定中。杜波依斯在他后来的作品《美国黑人的重建》中更清楚地解释了这一点："在剥削黑人无产阶级（黑人工人）的过程中，产生的剩余价值（利润）被人类的野兽窃取了。……人的解放是劳动的解放，劳动的解放就是对大多数黄种人、棕色人和黑人工人的解放。"[3]

时代贡献

杜波依斯对美国种族主义的分析是以由像弗雷德里克·道格拉斯这样的前奴隶领导的废奴运动的成果为基础的。杜波依斯再次呼吁进行社会斗争，这是对早期思想的延续，但他的方法更科学，融合了社会科学的最新发展成果，并将经济学与种族主义、不平等联系起来。

尽管杜波依斯借鉴了德国哲学家 G. W. F. 黑格尔等学者的研究成果，但他以一种新的方式论述了非裔美国人的身份。他将黑格尔的历史与意识之间的联系——以及对分裂人格的心理研究——运用到美国黑人的处境中。他指出白人种族主义导致黑人产生身份问题并阻碍了他们提升社会地位。他坚持认为消除压迫和不平等的最佳途径是社会冲突，而不是妥协（即简单接受种族主义行为）。杜波依斯强调教育、骄傲和领导能力，并以此鼓励黑人去推动美国人道主义社会的发展。

人们很容易把杜波依斯认为对黑人的剥削是为了美国白人的经济利益的观点与德国哲学家卡尔·马克思的观点相提并论。马克思认为，历史是以工人阶级和统治阶级之间的斗争为特征的。然而，杜波依斯明确表示，在他当时的学术生涯中，他对马克思主义 * 只有一个初步的了解。正如他所言，"（在我早期的作品中）有一些方法，一些间接提及，但没有完全将卡尔·马克思的哲学思想运用到我的研究课题中。马克思主义后来才出现，那时我开始深入研究社会现实，并在《美国黑人的重建》（1935）中达到了顶峰。"[4]

1. W. E. B. 杜波依斯：《黑人的灵魂》，纽约、伦敦：W.W. 诺顿出版公司，1999 年，第 221—346 页。

2. 例如，见格雷格·约翰逊："W. E. B. 杜波依斯的《费城黑人》"，载《宾州趋势》，2009 年 7 月 2 日，登录日期 2015 年 1 月 20 日，http://www.upenn.edu/pennnews/current/node/3997。

3. W. E. B. 杜波依斯：《美国黑人的重建》，纽约：罗素出版社，1963 年，第 16 页。

4. W. E. B. 杜波依斯：《对美利坚合众国的非洲奴隶贸易的平抑过程（1638—1870）》，纽约：社会科学出版社，1954 年，第 327—329 页。

第二部分：学术思想

5 思想主脉

要点 🔑

- 杜波依斯在《黑人的灵魂》中提出了三个核心概念："肤色界线"（种族主义）——20世纪美国面临的主要问题；"双重意识"——黑人在种族主义社会中试图同时作为非洲人和美国人的心理挑战；"面纱"——种族主义在白人和黑人之间制造的障碍。

- 作者希望有一天，美国社会将超越种族主义，实现民主，全人类将团结起来。

- 杜波依斯对亲身经历和亲眼目睹的种族主义深感悲痛，但他仍然乐观地认为，一个更加公正的社会必将出现。

核心主题

在《黑人的灵魂》的前言（"前思"）中，W. E. B. 杜波依斯说："这里掩埋着许多东西，如果你耐心地读下去，这些东西将会告诉你20世纪初作为黑人的奇特意义。亲爱的读者，这意义并非与你毫无关系；因为20世纪的问题是肤色界线的问题。"[1]

这段话将种族主义描述为美国社会的重大问题，是长期以来一直困扰着黑人和白人的问题。这是贯穿全书的主题。杜波依斯接着思考了这一问题如何影响了非裔美国人对自己所处社会的看法，并提出问题："人们对种族主义成为一个社会问题作何感想？"[2]

然后作者回答道："身为一个穷人很苦，但是在一个遍地美元的国度里，一个贫穷的种族则是最苦的。"[3]

杜波依斯接着讨论了内战、解放宣言、重建时期、吉姆·克劳法时期所实施的种族隔离和不平等所带来的遗留问题。在此，他强调了种族主义和资本主义之间的紧密联系。

杜波依斯描述了奴隶制和吉姆·克劳法是如何在非裔美国人的脑海中形成一种根深蒂固的印象的。为此，他引入了本书中两个最重要的概念：双重意识和面纱隐喻。

作者对反抗压迫的斗争持乐观态度。他强调了黑人领袖的重要性，与另一位杰出的黑人政治人物布克·T. 华盛顿不同，杜波依斯认为，非裔美国人必须参与社会斗争。他希望有一天，这场斗争会带来公民平等、选举权、教育平等以及建立一个以才能来评判人的精英体制。

> "这个民族还没有与自己的罪恶和解；自由人还没有在自由中找到他的福地。不管在这些变化的岁月里会有什么好事，极度失望的阴影一直笼罩着黑人。"
>
> —— W. E. B. 杜波依斯：《黑人的灵魂》

思想探究

"双重意识"一词描述了非裔美国人分裂的思想状态。这是由黑人每天面临的挑战造成的，他们一面试着融入主流的白人文化，同时又尽力保持对自己的黑人传统和身份的自豪感。杜波依斯把这种情况描述为："一个人感觉自己是双重性的，既是美国人，又是黑人；两个灵魂，两种思想，两股无法调和的力量：两种冲突的理想并存于一个黑色的躯体里，只有极其顽强的力量才能阻止自己被撕裂。"[4]

杜波依斯接着介绍了他的"面纱"隐喻，它代表了两个世界之间的分裂：一个是占统治地位的白人世界，另一个是在政治上、经济上和社会上都被边缘化的黑人世界。非裔美国人经常被白人的种族主义观点所阻碍，无法发挥自己的潜能。这种观点不仅歪曲了现实，而且对黑人造成精神上的折磨。如杜波依斯所说："在美国这个世界里，黑人……天生带着面纱，具有预见力，这个世界没有给他真正的自我意识，却只是让他透过另一个世界的启示来看自己……这是一种双重意识，一种总是通过别人的眼光看自己，带着轻蔑和怜悯来衡量一个人灵魂的感觉。"[5]

杜波依斯在写到这种双重意识时，谈到了自己作为一个黑人在白人世界中的经历，描述了他是如何"……被巨大的面纱隔绝在白人的世界外"。[6]他用他在菲斯克大学时的一个故事来说明他的观点，当时他想要给一个白人女孩一张贺卡，但那个白人女孩以他是黑人为由拒绝了。

杜波依斯描述了黑人对双重意识状态的三种反应。有人美化自己的黑色，以此来让自己感到骄傲（20世纪60年代的"黑即是美"*运动就是一个很好的例子）。有人通过反抗主流社会进行报复（如20世纪60年代的黑人权力*运动）。还有人努力改变自己来融入白人文化。

杜波依斯希望通过黑人的骄傲、教育、领导能力和斗争使黑人能够穿越面纱，克服双重意识带来的创伤。

语言表述

杜波依斯运用了多种文学创作手法，包括隐喻、自传、黑人灵歌、圣经典故和希腊神话，以说服两类截然不同的读者。第一类读者来自主流的白人社会，处在面纱的另一边，利用种族主义使非裔美国人边缘化。他谈到了黑人所遭受的不公正待遇，呼吁白人表现出更多的人性。第二类是站在面纱后面的黑人读者，他们受到吉姆·克劳法的压迫，希望从白人统治中解放出来。在一个种族主义和不平等的世界里，杜波依斯希望用一种预言的声音来引导和激励黑人读者，这种声音突显了非裔美国人丰富的文化、精神和斗争的历史。

除了这些文学手法之外，杜波依斯还将社会学和经济学联系起来，将科学方法应用到他的论证中。他特别强调了资本主义社会中白人的贪婪与黑人劳工所遭受的种族歧视和不平等之间的关系。

今天，"肤色界线""双重意识""面纱"等概念在社会学乃至其他领域中仍然非常重要。

---

1. 杜波依斯：《黑人的灵魂》，第 5 页。
2. 杜波依斯：《黑人的灵魂》，第 9 页。
3. 杜波依斯：《黑人的灵魂》，第 14 页。
4. 杜波依斯：《黑人的灵魂》，第 11 页。
5. 杜波依斯：《黑人的灵魂》，第 10—11 页。
6. 杜波依斯：《黑人的灵魂》，第 10 页。

6 思想支脉

要点 ✍

- 杜波依斯在文中提到了两个次要的主题。首先，在重建时期，进一步实现平等的进程遭到了对内战和废奴心怀怨恨的白人的破坏。第二，在吉姆·克劳法时期，宗教和黑人教会极大地鼓励了黑人的骄傲、反抗和斗争。

- 为帮助获得自由的奴隶融入白人社会所做的努力，如自由民局*等，经常遭到心怀不满的白人破坏。

- 在一个黑人受压迫的社会里，宗教和黑人教会为黑人提供了避难所，并成为集体反抗种族主义的灵感来源。

其他思想

W. E. B. 杜波依斯《黑人的灵魂》，耗时 7 年，是一部由 14 篇文章组成的合集，所以自然涉及到一些次要的主题。其中最重要的两个主题体现在《自由的曙光》和《我们父辈的信仰》中。

在《自由的曙光》中，杜波依斯探讨了自由民局。这个联邦政府机构在 1865 年至 1877 年的重建时期帮助被解放的奴隶融入白人社会。该机构由亚伯拉罕·林肯总统于 1865 年建立，通过提供教育服务、法律援助和就业机会来帮助黑人融入社会。然而，其努力在很大程度上受到了南方白人（比如暴力至上主义组织三 K 党*）的破坏，后者对内战的失败和奴隶制的废除怀恨在心。南方各州在 1865 年和 1866 年通过了继续推行白人至上的黑人法典*，这也阻碍了自由民局的工作。根据法典，一个人的血统中若存有任何黑人血统，则他们在法律上就是黑人。例如，公共设施的隔离意味着黑人不能使用为白人准备的盥洗室。自由人被迫工作，但他们不能学习读写，也不能在没有白人在场的情况下集会。这些法规旨在确保白人拥有稳定的廉价劳动力。其中包括流浪法规，这允许白人逮捕任何他们怀疑擅自离开工作场所的人；任何不能缴纳罚款的黑人都将被判强制劳动。1872 年，尤利西斯·格兰特 * 成为总统，他突然关闭了自由民局，因为美国南方反对帮助那些希望过上好日子的黑人。

《我们父辈的信仰》这篇文章描述了美国黑人教会的历史和影响，以及宗教如何塑造和影响了非裔美国人的文化和反抗。杜波依斯特别关注黑人牧师、过去为奴的黑人或奴隶的后代在促进黑人集体团结方面发挥过的重要作用。

> "身为一个穷人是苦的，但是在一个遍地美元的国度里，一个贫穷的种族则是最苦的。"
>
> ——W. E. B. 杜波依斯：《黑人的灵魂》

思想探究

杜波依斯在《自由的曙光》中提出了一个主要论点：尽管据称内战始于每个州与联邦相比应该拥有多少权力的问题，但这并不是战争的根本原因。对杜波依斯来说，真正的问题是奴隶制。他说："我们知道黑人奴隶制问题是这场战争的真正原因。"[1]

在对重建的分析中，杜波依斯认为，尽管自由民局是一个重要的倡议，但其职能经常遭到破坏。虽然它帮助解放的奴隶接受教育，使他们能够进入新建的黑人学校，如菲斯克大学，但腐败的官员通常会设法剥夺成功黑人的财产。正如他所解释的那样，"在一个奴隶制还没有衰落的混乱国度里，阻止强者肆意虐待弱者，阻止弱者因强者的失势而幸灾乐祸，是一项吃力不讨好、毫无希望的工作。"[2] 杜波依斯认为，尽管废除了奴隶制，但吉姆·克劳法和其他形式的种族主义实际上导致了对黑人的再次奴役。

在《我们父辈的信仰》一文中，杜波依斯强调了宗教作为非裔美国人团结力量的重要性。他强调牧师在打破"肤色界线"的斗争中发挥的领导作用，利用黑人的信仰和团结穿越"面纱"，走向自由和正义。

被忽视之处

杜波依斯的作品对种族和民族研究以及后殖民主义研究产生了深远的影响（后殖民主义研究分析了欧洲殖民主义的物质和文化遗产）。然而，正如罗伯特·沃瑟姆*教授和厄尔·赖特*教授等学者指出的那样，社会学家往往忽略了杜波依斯的影响。[3] 在当时的政治经济背景下，杜波依斯走在了时代的前面，用科学方法研究黑人境况，而他对美国社会的观点与当时认为黑人的地位是由于"他们劣等的生理特点"的观点完全不同。这些贡献使杜波依斯成为有史以来最杰出的社会学家之一。

后殖民主义学者，如保罗·吉尔罗伊*和霍米·K.巴巴*，将"黑人和白人之间的不平等关系如何影响身份认同"这一问题推到了风口浪尖。吉尔罗伊展示了杜波依斯的思想如何将美国乃至全世界黑人的经历联系了起来。正如杜波依斯自己所说："全世界人民，我们美国黑人向你们呼吁；我们在美国的遭遇不仅仅是美国的内部问题。这是一个基本的人性问题，一个民主问题，一个由于种族和肤色而遭受歧视的问题；因此，它需要你的关注和行动。没有任何一个国家可以强大到全世界都能够让它继续蓄意使自己的公民遭受不公正、残酷和不公平的对待。"4

1. 杜波依斯:《黑人的灵魂》，第 7 页。

2. 杜波依斯:《黑人的灵魂》，第 29—30 页。

3. 罗伯特·A. 沃瑟姆:"W. E. B. 杜波依斯的社会学概论"，载《今日社会》，2005 年第 3 期，第 1 页。厄尔·赖特:"W. E. B. 杜波依斯和亚特兰大社会学实验室"，载《今日社会》2005 年第 3 期，第 1 页。

4. 选自 W. E. B. 杜波依斯:《呼吁联合国纠正美国对剥夺黑人少数民族人权之声明》，纽约:全国有色人种协进会，1947 年。

7 历史成就

要点 ⚿━

- 杜波依斯质疑了美国社会的"种族主义的存在是因为黑人在生理上是低劣的"这一主流观点。他揭示了资本主义如何利用所谓的黑人种族劣等的观点来为廉价劳动力的合理性辩护。这种观点激起了全世界黑人的抗争。

- 杜波依斯不赞同马库斯·加维*更为激进的立场。马库斯呼吁美国黑人放弃自己的国家，回到自己祖先的家园。

- 杜波依斯的一生见证了黑人抗争的巨大进步，但他的全人类和谐相处的愿望并没有完全实现，因为种族主义仍然存在。

观点评价

作为一名学术研究者、教师、记者和活动家，杜波依斯通过强调美国和其他地方的资本主义贪婪与种族主义之间的联系，在全球范围内鼓励黑人斗争。他鼓励黑人为平等而战，不要为了一些基本的权利而接受白人的政治统治和歧视。黑人灵魂中最重要的三个概念——肤色界线、双重意识和面纱——继续对种族和民族研究以及后殖民主义研究产生着重要影响。

1903年，当时种族主义在美国社会普遍存在，但《黑人的灵魂》的面世立即产生了影响。仅在出版后的两个月，就已第三次印刷。虽然作者在此之前已经出版了两本书并发表了大量的学术和新闻文章，但这本书使他获得了国际上的认可。作家和文学评论家亨利·詹姆斯*等重要人物对这本书的文学价值和社会价值大加赞赏。但与此同时，包括另一位黑人领袖布克·T. 华盛顿在内的许多南方地区的名人批评杜波依斯挑起了"不必要"的争论。[1] 在 1903 年到 1940 年间，这本书在该地区售出了 2 万册。1953 年，纽约的蓝色苍鹭出版社出版发行了 1 000 册 50 周年纪念版，杜波依斯为这本书写了新的前言。2003 年，纪念活动在美国各地和其他地方举行了纪念活动，以表彰作者的贡献。[2] 尽管如此，杜波依斯的愿望并未完全实现，因为种族主义和不平等仍然存在。

> "他（杜波依斯）在自己身上体现了黑人的骄傲。他并没有因为自己是黑人并因此被当成残疾而道歉，相反，他攻击压迫者，因为他们的罪行阻碍了黑人的发展。他是勇敢和正直的典范，他敢于直面社会体制。尽管压迫者对他充满了怨恨和轻蔑，但他那有力的反抗之声却从未停止过。
>
> —— 马丁·路德·金博士

当时的成就

在曾为奴的弗雷德里克·道格拉斯的研究和社会行动的基础上，杜波依斯挑战了白人至上主义和布克·T. 华盛顿所持的"黑人应该接受歧视，以换取社会地位的有限提升"的立场。但他也反对马库斯·加维更为激进的立场。

加维是出生于牙买加的黑人民族主义者*，在 1914 年创立了世界黑人进步协会*。后来，他搬到了纽约的哈莱姆区，在那里他论证了黑人的纯洁性，主张与白人社会分离，并呼吁所有的美国黑人"回到"他们祖先的家园——非洲。尽管杜波依斯称赞加维提升了黑人的自豪感和自信，但他强烈反对加维的观点。杜波依斯认为黑人既是非洲人又是美国人，任何时候都不应该失去任一身份。他认为，如果黑人由知识界精英或者他称之为"十中有一的人才"*来领导，他们就可以在美国社会实现平等，同时保留他们丰富的遗产和文化身份。杜波依斯用"十中有一的人才"这个词来描述他最初的想法，即每十个黑人中就有一个能成为领袖，帮助他们的黑人同胞崛起。杜波依斯认为，为了净化压迫者和被压迫者的灵魂以达到人性的更高境界，必须历经黑人斗争、白人认同黑人身份的过程。

《黑人的灵魂》为更好地理解种族主义和黑人身份奠定了基础，为美国和昔日欧洲殖民地的未来黑人领袖和解放斗争提供了灵感。

尽管《黑人的灵魂》主张黑人享有平等的公民权利和政治权利，以及为黑人提供平等教育和建立精英制度，但自《黑人的灵魂》1903 年出版以来，其目标并没有完全实现。虽然如此，作者仍应作为历史上最重要的社会学家之一被铭记，因为他在提高全世界被压迫人民的地位方面发挥了重要作用。

局限性

《黑人的灵魂》首先适用于 19 世纪晚期和 20 世纪初美国的种族主义和身份问题。书中描述了一个以白人特权为基础、以白人种族至上主义为主导信念的社会。因此，黑人是二等公民。杜波依斯写的 14 篇文章涉及内战、奴隶制、重建、资本主义与种族主义的关联、种族主义对非裔美国人身份的影响、宗教与黑人教会、骄傲、反抗和斗争。该书还具有更广泛的意义，它突出展现了资本主义社会中白人压迫少数民族的方式，以及这种方式如何妨碍整个社会进步、阻碍民主发挥作用。《黑人的灵魂》应该

被视作是一部与多个学术研究领域相关的跨学科杰作，也是一部
超越时间的杰作。

---

1. W. E. B. 杜波依斯:《黑人的灵魂》, 纽约、伦敦：W.W. 诺顿出版公司, 1999 年
   版，第 221—346 页。
2. 麻省大学图书馆，特殊馆藏，大学档案，杜波依斯百科词典，2013 年 12 月 18
   日，登录日期 2015 年 1 月 20 日 http://scua.library.umass.edu/duboisopedia/doku.
   php?id=about:souls_of_black_folk。

8 著作地位

要点 🔑

- W. E. B.杜波依斯的所有著作都揭露了种族主义，强调了其对身份、意识、民主以及人性的影响，然后鼓励通过集体斗争来克服它。
- 《黑人的灵魂》是杜波依斯一生致力于增进人类理解所做努力的重要组成部分之一。
- 《黑人的灵魂》以杜波依斯之前的作品《费城黑人》为基础，使杜波依斯享誉全球。从此，他反抗压迫的斗争就具有了全球视角。

定位

1896 年，杜波依斯受雇于宾夕法尼亚大学，在那里他开始研究费城黑人的生活状况。这项研究在当时是非常先进的，融合了包括访谈、参与者观察、历史及数据分析等几种不同的方法。杜波依斯的传记作者大卫·利弗林·刘易斯 * 教授解释道："当杜波依斯列出 15 000 份家庭时间表时，在他面前呈现的是七区整个黑人人口的生活史，涵盖了近 10 000 人，包括男人、女人和孩子。"[1]

这一高强度的研究最后汇集成杜波依斯的第一部开创性著作《费城黑人》，他于 1899 年在亚特兰大大学工作期间出版了这本书。1903 年，杜波依斯出版了《黑人的灵魂》，这本书再次采用了多样的研究方法，进一步突显了美国的种族主义和不平等状况。这是一部成熟的作品，奠定了作者作为一位治学严谨的国内外学者的地位。

杜波依斯一生都坚信研究人员应该运用他们的科学研究给社会带来变革。1910 年，他离开了亚特兰大大学，转而领导全国有色

人种协进会。*

1920 年，他出版了《黑水：面纱里的声音》，这是他三部自传中的第一部。这本书讨论了全球范围内黑人受到的压迫，有一章是专门描写黑人女性的反抗斗争的。到那时为止，杜波依斯的愿景是泛非主义*的，甚至是普世的。他鼓励世界各地少数民族与压迫作斗争。

1935 年，他出版了《美国黑人的重建》，关注了重建期间不同的经济阶层。该书认为，19 世纪末和 20 世纪初白人和黑人工人未能团结起来反对压迫他们的白人有产者，导致了吉姆·克劳法的出台，剥夺了大多数黑人和许多贫穷白人的公民权。这样的观点挑战了"黑人应该为自己的不幸负责"的主流观点。在这部作品中，杜波依斯还展示了黑人反抗运动如何抵制了吉姆·克劳法和如何全面提升了美国的人性。

1950 年，杜波依斯代表纽约市竞选美国参议员，竞选立场是资本主义应该对全球的种族主义负责。虽然杜波依斯承认苏联*有许多缺点，但他为其社会主义的政治结构辩护，认为这是一种有潜力的解决办法。他之后竞选失败。1951 年，美国政府因杜波依斯日益激进的思想而对他进行审判，禁止他出境（禁令生效至 1958 年）。作为反抗，杜波依斯于 1961 年加入了美国共产党，两年后移居加纳。加纳曾是英国的殖民地，那时刚刚获得独立。他成了一名加纳公民，继续与来自西非的全球种族主义作斗争。

> "杜波依斯告诉读者，种族主义和歧视不仅阻碍了黑人发展，而且对白人产生了严重的负面影响，白人对黑人的恐惧、怀疑、不信任、蔑视和仇恨削弱了他们自身的人性。因此，种族主义的遗留问题使整个国家缺乏基本的人性修养，而美国本应是在这一基础上建立的。"
>
> ——桑德拉·L. 巴恩斯教授，范德比尔特大学

整合

作为一名学者、记者和活动家，杜波依斯毕生致力于挑战种族主义和克服不平等问题来提升黑人在美国的社会地位。他的第一部影响深远的作品《费城黑人》写于 1899 年，使他对黑人在追求平等时所面临的挑战有了深刻的认识。正如他所说，"仅靠出生在一个群体中并不一定就能对这个群体有全面的了解。"[2] 他生活在美国南部被剥夺公民权的黑人之中，成了一名研究非裔美国人生活中许多不同方面的研究者和教师。

虽然杜波依斯在 1903 年写《黑人的灵魂》时还不太了解马克思主义，但他分析了种族主义的政治经济，并将其视为资本主义的副产品。他还谈到种族主义对黑人和白人身份形成所造成的影响。杜波依斯将"肤色界线"定义为 20 世纪的重要分水岭，并引入了他的开创性概念"双重意识"和"面纱"。此外，他强调教育和领导能力对取得平等公民身份的重要性。

32 年后的 1935 年，在写《美国黑人的重建》时，杜波依斯对马克思主义有了全面的了解，并且深入探讨了工业经济和种族主义之间的关系。在大萧条 * 的背景下——从 1929 年到 1939 年的全球经济危机——他详细描述了工业资本主义如何创造了一个有利于白人有产者而非工人的制度，以及特权阶级是如何利用种族主义这个工具扩充财富的。他还质疑了"黑人在重建期间未能得到解放是因为黑人在政治和社会其他领域都不成功"的主流观点。与人们普遍的观点不同，他认为，在内战之后，北方并不是"宽宏大量的解放者"，而南方也不是"命中注定的殉道者"。[3] 杜波依斯认为，奴隶制是内战的主要原因，而随后的吉姆·克劳法是白人故意强加给黑人以维护自身利益的一种制度。

显然，随着时间的推移，杜波依斯对俄国革命*、冷战*等重大世界事件以及亲身遭遇的种族主义和不平等的反应变得更加激进。但他所有的作品都因他为争取民主和人道精神进步而联结在了一起。

意义

杜波依斯一生对学术界和社会做出了巨大的贡献。他撰写了21本书，主编了15本书，发表了100多篇论文和文章。[4] 他还是黑人民权组织尼亚加拉运动*、全国有色人种协进会和泛非主义（是一种鼓励全世界非洲人民团结的思想意识）的领导人。《黑人的灵魂》只是他一生为平等而奋斗所做的重要贡献之一。

杜波依斯的学术研究虽然通常与社会学相关，但其实是涵盖了多个学科的跨学科研究。1897年，在美国政治和社会科学院的一次会议上，他认为有必要将历史研究、数据分析、人类学测量数据（直接向人们收集的有关人类生活方式的数据）与社会学解释相结合，从不同的角度来研究"非裔美国人问题"。杜波依斯的学术成就对社会学、历史学、经济学、政治学、宗教研究、艺术和文学产生了重要影响。

目前，杜波依斯的研究融汇了非裔美国人研究、种族与民族研究以及后殖民主义研究。像保罗·吉尔罗伊和霍米·K.巴巴这样的重要学者发扬了他关于种族主义和黑人身份的观点，并将其应用到更广泛的全球背景中以应对反殖民斗争、去殖民化（即废除殖民主义）和后殖民时期移民等问题。作者的观点在学术界仍然很重要，并且继续激励着全球的社会运动。

1. 大卫·利弗林·刘易斯：《W. E. B. 杜波依斯：1868—1919 年的种族传记》，纽约：亨利·霍尔特出版社，1993 年，第 191 页。

2. W. E. B. 杜波依斯：《W. E. B. 杜波依斯自传》，纽约：国际出版社，1968 年，第 198 页。

3. W. E. B. 杜波依斯：《美国黑人的重建》，纽约：罗素出版社，1963 年，第 723 页。

4. 全国有色人种协进会史：W. E. B. 杜波依斯，登录日期 2015 年 1 月 28 日，http://www.naacp.org/pages/naacp-history-W. E. B.-dubois。

第三部分：学术影响

9 最初反响

要点 &—

- 一些匿名的评论家称赞《黑人的灵魂》具有伟大的文学价值和社会价值。一些人对此书褒贬不一，难下定论。而更多的人认为这是一部危险之作，因为它会加剧种族间的紧张关系。

- 1904 年，此书出版一年后，W. E. B. 杜波依斯承认《黑人的灵魂》有一些小的瑕疵，但他仍然坚持书中表达的所有观点。

- 影响人们对这本书看法的最重要因素是其写作时期——吉姆·克劳法时期。

批评

W. E. B. 杜波依斯的《黑人的灵魂》大胆质疑了"黑人在生理上和文化上都不如白人，黑人要为自己在重建中解放的失败负责"的主流观点。就像杜波依斯的其他作品一样，它用强有力的论据证明了这种观点与事实之间的巨大鸿沟。

《黑人的灵魂》发表后，立即收到了褒贬不一的反应。一方面，有些人称赞《黑人的灵魂》的文学和社会价值，比如《国家》杂志的一位匿名评论员就表达了他对该书的情感力量和它对读者吸引力的敬仰之情。《卫理公会杂志和评论》的另一篇文章称赞了杜波依斯"出色的文采"，而来自《威斯敏斯特评论》的评论家则认为，"这部作品为长期困扰美国的种族问题提供了合理的解决方案。"[1]

另一方面，一些人把此书视为威胁，认为它会加剧种族间的紧张关系。一位匿名的评论家在《纳什维尔美国人》中写道：

"对于黑人来说，读这本书确实很危险，因为它只会激起不满和种族仇恨，用不存在的或者不应该在意的东西来满足他的想象力。"《纽约时报》的另一位匿名评论员指责杜波依斯攻击布克·T.华盛顿，并且认为，作为一个北方黑人，杜波依斯不应该为南方代言。[2]

而其他评论者则表达了较为暧昧的意见。《美国评论月刊》的一位匿名评论员写道，"近年来出版的该类书籍，没有任何一本能与这一小书的力量或优美表达相媲美，"但接着又说，"作为黑人教育问题的一种实际解决方案，他的文章不足以与华盛顿先生广泛发表的演讲和演说相提并论。"[3]

> "正如杜波依斯在'后记'中所暗示的那样，他曾十分担心这本书'落于荒野，无人问津'，但是这一担心很快烟消云散了。"
>
> —— 大卫·利弗林·刘易斯教授，纽约大学

回应

1904年，杜波依斯在《独立报》上发表了对自己著作的评论。虽然他没有直接回应批评，但他确实反思和回顾了《黑人的灵魂》。他为书中某些章节的唐突而道歉，并解释说，因为他花了七年的时间写了这本书，所以他混合了不同的风格、语调和观点。尽管如此，杜波依斯还是坚持自己的观点，并明确指出，将14篇文章联结在一起的是这样一个思想：美国是一个种族主义根深蒂固的国家，并且这种种族主义必须被克服。[4]

杜波依斯和华盛顿之间关于黑人反对种族主义和不平等时该持

有的导向的争论一直持续到 1915 年华盛顿去世。杜波依斯坚持认为，只有教育、领导能力、反抗和斗争才能给美国社会带来平等。他特别强调需要像他这样受过高等教育的黑人来引导大众改变社会。虽然杜波依斯的观点随着时间的推移变得更加激进，但他作品的本质始终如一。

冲突和共识

杜波依斯出版《黑人的灵魂》的历史时期影响了该书的接受程度。尽管一些激进分子称赞杜波依斯在文学和社会方面的卓越表现，但很多南方白人批评他挑战当时那种使白人享有特权，并允许他们扩大财富的现状。[5]

南方的白人把黑人政治发言人布克·T. 华盛顿看作盟友，因为他接受"白人天生优越、黑人应该服从他们"的观点。作为总统顾问，华盛顿对黑人教育有一定的财政控制，并在掌握权力的白人中享有良好的声誉，他们认为他可以帮助他们，使社会接受继续剥削黑人的行为。

杜波依斯把华盛顿处理种族主义的方式称为塔斯基吉机器。阿拉巴马州的塔斯基吉是华盛顿建立黑人大学的地方，此举是为了改善非裔美国人的生活。杜波依斯不同意华盛顿的看法，即与白人合作是战胜种族主义的途径，但他承认，要打倒华盛顿的势力是非常困难的。正如杜波依斯所言："大多数报纸都发现，不反对华盛顿先生对他们有利，即使他们并不完全同意他的观点。那些谋求高位的黑人也卑躬屈膝地巴结他。"[6]

然而，杜波依斯通过他的著作、教学和行动，确实挑战了华盛顿作为当时黑人领袖的地位。凭借自身的说服力和基于科学的论点，杜波依斯成功地让一些白人对美国的情况有所反思，并为美国和其他地方的黑人进步提供了灵感和动力。

1. W. E. B. 杜波依斯：《黑人的灵魂》，纽约、伦敦：W. W. 诺顿出版公司，1999年，第 xx 页，第 221—234 页。

2. 杜波依斯：《黑人的灵魂》，第 26 页。

3. 艾伯特·肖："新书：美国近期出版物的注释"，载《美国每月评论》第 28 卷，1903 年，第 249 页。

4. W. E. B. 杜波依斯："黑人的灵魂"，载《独立报》第 57 卷，1904 年，第 2920 页。

5. 杜波依斯：《黑人的灵魂》，第 221—234 页。

6. W. E. B. 杜波依斯：《黎明的黄昏：对一个种族自传的随笔》，纽约：赫考特·布雷斯出版社，1940 年，第 76 页。

10 后续争议

要点 🔑

- 《黑人的灵魂》和W. E. B.杜波依斯的其他著作都对吉姆·克劳法时代美国的种族主义进行了详细的分析，鼓励为平等而斗争。这在美国和其他地方都产生了重大影响。

- 今天，杜波依斯的思想遗产融汇了黑人政治思想、种族与民族研究以及后殖民主义研究。

- 他的学术成就影响了保罗·吉尔罗伊和霍米·K.巴巴等著名学者的思想。两人都将他的"双重意识"概念应用到后殖民主义研究中，进一步扩展了这个概念。

应用和问题

W. E. B.杜波依斯《黑人的灵魂》中三个关键的概念是"肤色界线"、"双重意识"和"面纱"。

在杜波依斯的一生中，他对"肤色界线"的看法发生了变化。在1952年的《黑人与华沙犹太人区》[1]一书中，他解释说，直到他亲眼目睹第二次世界大战*期间犹太人在华沙犹太人区*的生活，他才完全理解美国黑人的处境，而在1903年，他将其狭义地描述为划分白人和黑人的标志。正如杜波依斯所说：

"在我看来，美国的奴隶制、解放和阶层制度不再是我长久以来设想的一个独立存在且独特的问题。它甚至不仅仅是肤色、身体和种族特征的问题……不，我感兴趣的种族问题跨越了肤色、体格、信仰和地位的界限，其根源在于文化模式、被歪曲的教义和人类的仇恨与偏见，这些触及了各种各样的人，给所有的人带来无尽的不幸。"[2]

这段引文很重要，因为它表明杜波依斯如何渐渐理解了种族主义不仅仅是分裂美国白人和黑人之间的"面纱"。相反，它表明了他对种族主义更深刻的理解，即种族主义是一个随着时间的推移而不断变化的现象。从那时起，从汉娜·阿伦特*到保罗·吉尔罗伊等形形色色的学者开始研究种族主义的本质以及它与其他形式的歧视（比如反犹太主义*和性别歧视）的关系。

杜波依斯在 1897 年的《黑人的奋斗》中首次使用了"双重意识"一词，然后在《黑人的灵魂》中进一步拓展了这一概念。它指的是在一个种族主义根深蒂固的社会中，一个人同时作为非洲人和美国人的身份冲突。正如杜波依斯所言，"（非裔美国人）只是想让既为黑人又为美国人的双重身份得以实现，不会因此被他的同胞诅咒和唾骂，也不会让机会之门在他面前被粗暴地关上。"[3]

杜波依斯用"面纱"这个词作为隐喻来描述这两种意识（非洲人和美国人）和两个社会（白人和黑人）之间的区别。他认为，这种"肤色界线"既是祸，也是福，是一种可以通过斗争和认同来消除的危险。

许多学者将杜波依斯的"肤色界线"和"面纱"比喻运用到其他语境中。在马提尼克出生的非裔法国作家、革命家弗朗茨·法农*就是一个突出的例子。他在 1952 年的开创性作品《黑皮肤，白面具》中使用了这些概念来阐述白人殖民者对黑人身份的理解。在一篇文章中，法农描述了一个白人男孩看到法农，指着他说，"看，一个黑人！"然后跳进妈妈的怀里寻找安全。经历了这一切，法农痛苦地否认了自己的身份。他说："在那个白色的冬日里，我的身体被撕开、扭曲、重新上色，穿着丧服。"[4]

这段描述与杜波依斯第一次遭遇身为黑人的尴尬相似。当他向菲斯克大学的白人女孩送贺卡时，对方拒绝接受。杜波依斯写道：

"突然间，我意识到我和其他人是不一样的；或者在内心、生活和期盼中（可能）和他们一样，却被一面巨大的面纱隔绝在了他们的世界之外。"[5]

> "尽管我们的社会比以往任何时候都更加宽容，但存在一种新的种族主义形式——令人厌恶的种族主义。其特征是平等主义态度，却对黑人采取回避和微妙的歧视。黑人继续面临双重意识的困境。如康奈尔·韦斯特（1993）所言，研究证实'种族'在机会、权利、待遇和生活质量方面仍然很重要。"
>
> —— 桑德拉·L. 巴恩斯教授，范德堡大学

思想流派

1903 年时，杜波依斯属于两个学派。首先，他对以证据为基础的社会学的发展做出了重大贡献，因为他解释了吉姆·克劳法背景下种族主义的物质原因以及导致不平等的成因。第二，反对布克·T. 华盛顿，捍卫社会斗争与平等。杜波依斯继承了前人的传统，像弗雷德里克·道格拉斯一样反对奴隶制。杜波依斯是主张取消种族隔离的人，这意味着他相信，通过社会冲突，白人和黑人社会最终可以统一为一个多元文化的团体，民主和人性将蓬勃发展。从这个意义上说，他是马丁·路德·金的先驱，但他发现自己与马库斯·加维的分离主义观点不一致。后者为 20 世纪 60 年代倡导黑

人分裂主义的黑人权力运动开辟了舞台。

今天，杜波依斯的作品融汇了黑人政治思想、种族与种族研究以及后殖民主义研究。他所有的作品都聚焦于种族主义以及被压迫者如何超越"肤色界线"。他的晚期作品，比如 1961 年的《有色人种的世界》，通过呼吁结束与资本主义密切相关的殖民统治和全球帝国主义，在美国国内外产生了很大影响。

当代研究

杜波依斯影响了许多当代学者，尤其是保罗·吉尔罗伊和霍米·K.巴巴。在吉尔罗伊的作品《黑大西洋》中，他将杜波依斯对"双重意识"的描述扩展到了全世界的非洲后裔。他关注的是这些人如何成为历史不可分割的一部分，却又被暴力地排除在历史之外。他说，非裔在科学、文学、政治、社会和文化方面为社会做出了巨大的贡献，但白人把他们视作低人一等，不让他们享有白人的自由或完全的公民身份。今天的黑人知识分子能够质疑不公正，而且拥有吉尔罗伊所说的"一种清晰独到的视野"或"极度的客观性"。这些黑人知识分子的声音一直在与美国种族主义和欧洲殖民主义作斗争，并成功地质疑了"理性的、西方的进步"的主导论点——西方白人文化天生优越的观念。[6]

在《文化的定位》中，霍米·K.巴巴也以杜波依斯的"双重意识"概念为基础，认为第三个空间已经出现。在这个空间里，个体进化出的身份由不止一种背景或文化组成。这超越了杜波依斯提出的二分观点，即要么是黑人要么是白人，两者之间绝无其他。巴巴认为，打破这些严格的壁垒意味着"殖民者"和"被殖民者"之间的不断交流，最终将通向进步和更广的人性。

1. W. E. B. 杜波依斯："黑人和华沙犹太人区"，载《犹太人的生活》，1952 年 5 月。

2. W. E. B. 杜波依斯："杜波依斯的社会理论，黑人和华沙犹太人区"；菲尔·祖克曼：《犹太人的生活》，千橡市：派因福格出版社，2004 年，第 45—46 页。

3. W. E. B. 杜波依斯：《黑人的灵魂》，纽约、伦敦：W. W. 诺顿出版公司，1999 年，第 10—11 页。

4. 弗朗茨·法农：《黑皮肤，白面具》，伦敦：麦克吉本与基，1968 年，第 113 页。

5. 杜波依斯：《黑人的灵魂》，第 10 页。

6. 保罗·吉尔罗伊：《黑大西洋：现代性与双重意识》，伦敦：维尔森，1993 年，第 29，38—39，171 页。

11 当代印迹

要点

- 《黑人的灵魂》仍然是多个学科中具有开创性的范本。
- 该书持续向种族主义和不平等发起挑战，鼓励人们与之斗争。
- 总的来说，今天这本书向任何一个种族主义者或对种族主义持非批判态度的人都提出了挑战。

地位

1999 年和 2003 年，人们分别举行了 W. E. B. 杜波依斯《费城黑人》[1] 与《黑人的灵魂》[2]100 周年纪念活动。2005 年，由杜波依斯于 1905 年创立的黑人民权组织“尼亚加拉运动”[3] 举行了百年庆典。此外，2009 年，美国总统奥巴马在由杜波依斯联合创办的全国有色人种协进会[4]100 周年纪念活动上发表了讲话。伴随这些里程碑式的庆祝活动而来的还有一些学术期刊和书籍的出版，[5] 以及来自报纸和杂志（如《纽约时报》）的媒体报道。[6] 所有这些都突显出杜波依斯在很大程度上仍然是种族、种族主义、身份、民主、平等以及人权讨论的重要部分，甚至是一种激励。

2003 年，全国黑人艺术节在亚特兰大举办，纪念受杜波依斯启发的音乐、戏剧和其他艺术作品。[7] 同年，著名剧作家苏拉妮·戴维斯 * 在纽约城市大学的研究生中心主办了戏剧朗诵会，由演员丹尼·格洛弗等名人主诵《黑人的灵魂》的不同段落。[8] 显然，现在的人们对发扬和重新审视杜波依斯的作品仍很感兴趣。

> "非裔美国人的'二重性',即他们的双重意识,推动了自我碎片化概念的产生,这是现代主义的一个定义条件。认为'所有的身份都具有多重性'的观点曾被视为大胆鲁莽的,而现在已经是司空见惯的事了。探究特定的事物来展示普遍性,当然是经典之举。杜波依斯通过他出奇强大的文字,使黑人的特殊性变成了一种隐喻,一种人类处境的普遍现象。正因如此,《黑人的灵魂》才能持续向今天的新一代读者发出如此强烈的声音。"
>
> —— 小亨利·路易斯·盖茨教授,哈佛大学

互动

1903 年,《黑人的灵魂》初版时,杜波依斯对白人至上主义和布克·T.华盛顿以及他的支持者的妥协立场提出了挑战。总的来说,今天这本书向任何一个种族主义者或对种族主义持非批判态度的人都提出了挑战。杜波依斯认为种族主义是白人为了自己的物质利益而实施的社会建构。非批判立场的例子包括:认为是"多元文化主义"造成了社会动荡;看不清骚乱的根源,认为少数民族应该为他们所面临的歧视负责;断言西方社会已经发展至"后种族主义"的程度;以及,认为不同种族遭受的差别对待已不再重要。

这本书仍然是学者、记者和活动人士的重要参考,他们希望了解和解释以下问题:

- 种族主义的成因
- 种族主义如何塑造身份
- 不平等
- 少数民族教育和领导能力的重要性

- 宗教和精神在促成集体反抗方面的作用
- 全球少数民族斗争的遗产

持续争议

今天，杜波依斯仍然对种族与民族研究以及后殖民主义研究有很大影响。"肤色界线"、"双重意识"和"面纱"仍然是这些领域的重要主题。例如，心理学教授约翰·F. 多维迪奥*和塞缪尔·L. 盖特纳*就已经谈到，自杜波依斯出版《黑人的灵魂》以来，对种族主义的探讨发生了怎样的变化。他们指出，种族主义在西方已经变得更加微妙，并且经常伪装在多元文化主义、反种族主义和平等主义的言论中。[9]

美国社会学家 E. 富兰克林·弗雷泽*也是有关种族主义问题的作者，他认为杜波依斯笔下"肮脏破旧、饮食起居气息浓重、通风不畅、一贫如洗的乡村小屋"，[10] 就相当于今天城市里种族隔离严重、肮脏和缺乏机会的贫民窟。[11]

其他学者如道格拉斯·梅西*和南希·丹顿*表示，基于肤色的种族歧视一直持续到今天，尤其表现为当代美国黑人在教育和就业领域所面临的歧视程度。他们主张进行经济改革，以缓解社会下层非裔美国人日益增长的焦虑感。[12] 美国哲学家、公共知识分子康奈尔·韦斯特*曾问：为什么像杜波依斯这样杰出的黑人领袖如此之少？[13]

非裔美国研究专家安德鲁·布林斯利*[14] 和活动家埃里克·林肯*[15] 等学者已经指出了宗教在《黑人的灵魂》中的重要性，以及这本书对追求更加高尚人性的重视。两人都认为黑人教会是一个被忽视的工作领域。他们强调了黑人教会的历史作用，这些教会提供了教育机会、经济援助、庇佑，以及团结黑人集体以抵制种族主义、黑帮、毒品和贫困等。他们还强调了黑人教会在帮助塑造马丁·路德·金这样的黑人领袖方面的重要作用。所有这一切都表明《黑人的灵魂》的中心主题依然与现代学术研究息息相关。

---

1. 例如，见林恩·伯布里奇："作为经济分析师的 W. E. B. 杜波依斯：《费城黑人》100 周年纪念感想"，载《黑人政治经济学评论》第 26 卷，1999 年第 3 期，第 13—31 页。

2. 这里有太多例子可引。纪念活动在美国各地举行。

3. 例如，见帕特丽夏·多诺万："纪念尼亚加拉运动百年纪念活动"，载《布法罗大学记者》，2005 年 7 月 7 日，登录日期 2015 年 1 月 29 日，http://www.buffalo.edu/ubreporter/archive/vol36/vol36n41/articles/NiagaraMovement.html?print=1。

4. "总统在全国有色人种协进会百年纪念大会上的讲话"，白宫新闻秘书办公室，2009 年 7 月 17 日，登录日期 2015 年 1 月 28 日，http://www.whitehouse.gov/the-press-office/remarks-president-naacp-centennial-convention-07162009。

5. 例如，见多兰·哈伯德：《黑人的灵魂：100 年后》，哥伦比亚：密苏里大学出版社，2007 年。

6. 亨利·路易斯·盖茨（小）："黑人的灵魂 100 周年：现在的两面"，载《纽约时报》，2003 年 5 月 4 日，登录日期 2015 年 1 月 18 日，http://www.nytimes.com/2003/05/04/books/review/04GATEST.html。

7. 泰瑞莎·斯托瓦尔："庆祝 W. E. B. 杜波依斯和流散艺术节"，载《危机》第 110 卷，2003 年第 5 期，第 48 页。

8. 新闻发布："'《黑人的灵魂》百年庆典'——在研究生中心首次举行以杜波依斯的经典作品为特色的戏剧朗读"，2003 年 1 月 1 日，登录日期 2015 年 1 月 28 日，http://www.gc.cuny.edu/News/GC-News/Detail?id=5920。

9. 约翰·F. 多维迪奥和塞缪尔·L. 盖特纳："令人生厌的种族主义形式"，《偏见、歧视和种族主义》，约翰·F. 多维迪奥和塞缪尔·L. 盖特纳编，奥兰多：学术出版社，1986 年，第 61—89 页。

10. 杜波依斯：《黑人的灵魂》，第 91 页。

11. E. 弗兰克林·弗雷泽：《美国的黑人教会》，利物浦：利物浦大学出版社，1964 年。

12. 道格拉斯·梅西和南希·登顿：《美国种族隔离：种族隔离与下层阶级的形成》，马萨诸塞州剑桥：哈佛大学出版社，1993 年。

13. 康奈尔·韦斯特："黑人知识分子的困境"，载《评论季刊》第 29 卷，1987 年第 4 期，第 39—52 页。

14. 安德鲁·布林斯利：《强大如河：黑人教会和社会改革》，纽约：牛津大学出版社，1999 年。

15. 埃里克·林肯：《种族、宗教和持续的美国困境》，纽约：希尔与王出版社，1984 年。

12 未来展望

要点 🔑

- 《黑人的灵魂》有望继续影响黑人研究、种族与民族研究以及后殖民主义研究。杜波依斯或仍将是全球社会运动的重要灵感来源。

- 杜波依斯的核心概念——"肤色界线"、"双重意识"和"面纱"——可能会继续作为进一步研究的重要参考点。

- 这本书之所以具有开创性，是因为它提升了我们对种族主义、种族主义对身份认同的影响以及如何共同努力克服种族主义的理解。

潜力

2003 年，人们组织了大规模的活动来纪念《黑人的灵魂》出版一百周年。在现代学术研究中，W. E. B. 杜波依斯的作品与种族和民族研究以及后殖民主义研究有很强的联系。这表明，这本书和杜波依斯的其他作品未来将继续发挥重要作用。尽管处在美国历史的特定背景，尤其是吉姆·克劳法的时代，但是作者对美国种族主义、利欲熏心世界里的种族主义根源、种族主义对身份认同的影响的见解，和他对美国有朝一日能改变"肤色界线"来实现真正的民主、获得更广的人性的希望，却是永恒的。这些核心问题不仅在今天的美国仍然具有重要意义，而且适用范围也更加广泛。在未来，学者们可能会继续将杜波依斯与历史上黑人和其他少数民族所面临的歧视和不平等，以及他们为克服这些所做的努力联系起来。

虽然《黑人的灵魂》的背景是美国社会，但以 1928 年小说《黑公主》为终曲的杜波依斯后来的作品，表达了他泛非主义的平等愿景。正如他所说，"非洲，当然，是我的祖国……有一件事是确定的，也是事实。那就是自 15 世纪以来，我的这些祖先就有了共同的历史，遭受了共同的灾难，有着长久的共同记忆……除了作为一种徽章，肤色的标记是相对不重要的；这种纽带关系的真正本质是奴隶制的遗留问题；歧视和侮辱……正是这二者的统一吸引我来到非洲。"[1]

> "杜波依斯明白改变将如何到来，后来的马丁·路德·金和所有民权领袖都明白这一点。他们明白不公正的法律需要被推翻；立法需要通过；总统需要受到一定压力才会采取行动。他们知道奴隶制的污点和种族隔离的罪恶必须在法庭和立法机构中消除。但他们也知道，在美国，变革必须来自人民……因为他们的行动，我们现在才是一个更加完美的联邦。"
>
> —— 美国总统巴拉克·奥巴马

未来方向

尽管随着时间的推移，社会运动已经取得了很大的进展，"肤色界线"仍然是 21 世纪的一个主要问题，当然它的性质随政治、经济、社会和文化的变化而改变。今天，美国种族主义的主要特征是阶级、肤色、宗教和性别等因素之间的联系。正如杜波依斯在第二次世界大战期间看到华沙犹太人聚居区的情况时所说的那样，种族主义是一种比他在早期作品中所描述的更为广泛和复杂的现象。通过他自己从马萨诸塞州的大巴灵顿到加纳的个人历程，他的观点愈加成熟，他也更好地更全面地理解了种族主义。在未来，学生、学者、记者和活动人士可能会继续探讨这一主题及其与身份形成、人权、反抗、斗争和协商之间的联系。那些研究种族与民族以及后殖民主义的学者，如保罗·吉尔罗伊和霍米·K.巴巴，就是例子。然而，作为一部跨学科著作，该书影响着不同领域的学术研究，并可能从其他领域（如宗教研究）中获得更多的关注。

小结

对于想更好地了解美国和非裔美国人历史的人来说，《黑人的灵魂》是一本必读著作。杜波依斯以曾经为奴的弗雷德里克·道格拉斯的思想遗产为基础，对奴隶制、美国内战、《解放宣言》、重建时期和吉姆·克劳法时期的种族歧视等问题进行了详尽、科学的分析。尽管在美国宪法第十三、十四和十五修正案中，黑人拥有选举权和其他重要的自由，但吉姆·克劳法最终还是重新奴役了黑人。

本书还对"种族这一社会建构是增加白人经济利益的手段"提供了重要的见解，对当时"黑人在生理和文化上不如白人"的主流观点提出了质疑。它还详细描述了种族主义对黑人身份的影响。

在《黑人的灵魂》一书中，杜波依斯致力于成为"黑人事业"的新领袖，鼓励黑人为自己的文化感到自豪，并从自己的精神世界中汲取灵感。他推动黑人集体参与社会斗争，使白人看到他们过去的不公正，从而承认黑人是平等的。杜波依斯希望通过这种方式，非裔美国人最终能够揭开"面纱"，战胜"双重意识"的折磨，帮助白人使美国成为其所宣称的"伟大的民主国家"，即"上帝庇佑下的一个不可分割的国家"。

这本书中最重要的三个概念——"肤色界线"、"双重意识"和"面纱"——很可能在未来很长的一段时间内都将是社会学乃至人类学、历史学、经济学和政治学等许多领域的基本概念。这本书很可能仍然是种族和民族研究以及后殖民主义分析的核心，主要原因是在资本主义背景下的种族主义继续存在并影响身份认同。如杜波依斯在 1903 年令人信服地论证的那样，只有通过教育、领导能力和社会冲突，才能克服种族主义。这些问题可能已经微妙地或以其他方式发生了变化，但"肤色界线"仍然是 21 世纪的一大问题。

---

1. W. E. B. 杜波依斯：《黎明的黄昏：对一个种族自传的随笔》，纽约：赫考特布雷斯出版社，1940 年，第 116 页。

术语表

1. **废除（奴隶制）**：指美国奴隶制的终结。

2. **废奴运动**：在美国内战结束奴隶制之前的运动。

3. **内战**：1861 年至 1865 年，美国北部（联邦）和南部（邦联）之间的战争。

4. **反犹太主义**：对犹太人的偏见或敌意。

5. **亚特兰大妥协案**：1895 年在亚特兰大达成的一项协议，规定黑人将服从白人种族主义和政治统治，以换取基本的法律权利和基础教育。

6. **《大西洋月刊》**：1857 年在波士顿创办，是美国历史最悠久、最权威的杂志之一。

7. **黑即是美**：20 世纪 60 年代在美国兴起的文化运动，旨在打破"黑人的外貌不如白人"的迷思。

8. **黑人法典**：前邦联州通过的法律，目的是限制被解放了的黑人的活动，并确保在废除奴隶制之后他们仍可作为随时可用的劳动力。

9. **黑人民族主义**：认为黑人应该脱离白人社会而自治的观点。

10. **黑人权力**：20 世纪 60 年代在美国兴起的一场政治运动，鼓励黑人分裂主义。

11. **资本主义**：强调生产资料私有制的经济制度。杜波依斯认为资本主义和种族主义之间联系密切。

12. **教化使命**：欧洲殖民主义奉行的信条，声称欧洲有责任教化"不文明的人"，从而为自己对殖民地的剥削辩护。

13. **冷战**：1945 年至 1990 年华约成员国（苏联及其盟国）与北约成员国之间存在的政治敌对状态。

14. **共产主义**：一种基于生产方式的国家所有制、劳动集体化和消灭社会阶级的政治意识形态。

15. **国会**：美国的国家立法机构，由参议院和众议院组成。1870 年，国会通过了宪法第十五修正案，授予非裔美国人选举权。

16. **意识**：根据黑格尔的观点，意识是他人对自己的认识的一种认识。换言之，我们通过别人的眼睛看自己。

17. **宪法**：一套公认的建立国家的原则。1787 年签署的美国宪法取代了邦联条款，建立了一个更强大的中央政府。

18. **《人权宣言》**：法国国民制宪会议于 1789 年签署的一份文件。它强调所有人生而平等，因此依法享有平等权利。

19. **哀歌**：表达哀悼和崇敬的诗歌。

20. **《解放奴隶宣言》**：亚伯拉罕·林肯总统于 1863 年内战中期发表的政治宣言。它规定，在反叛的南方各州，所有被当作奴隶的人从那一刻起都将获得自由。

21. **启蒙运动**：17 世纪和 18 世纪的一场文化和知识运动，旨在通过运用理性来改革社会。这为赫伯特·斯宾塞和查尔斯·达尔文的研究提供了"科学"背景，他们认为黑人在生理和文化上都不如白人。

22. **进化生物学**：学术研究的一个领域，涉及产生地球生物多样性的进化过程。W. E. B. 杜波依斯出版《黑人的灵魂》时，社会科学的主流观点是"黑人在生理上不如白人"。

23. **自由民局**：1865 年至 1872 年期间的联邦机构，通过为解放的奴隶提供教育服务、法律咨询和就业援助，帮助他们融入社会。

24. **法国大革命**：法国的政治和社会动荡时期，始于 1789 民众推翻君主制，终于 1799 年拿破仑的崛起。

25. **大萧条**：自 1929 年到第二次世界大战的全球金融危机。

26. **伟人理论**：一种认为伟人利用他们的天分、智慧、魅力和政治敏锐性来改变历史的理论。

27. **吉姆·克劳法时期**：美国历史上从 1877 年重建结束到 1950 年代和 1960 年代民权运动结束的一段时期。州和联邦政府制定了一些法律来阻止黑人获得更多平等。杜波依斯在那时出版了《黑人的灵魂》。

28. **三 K 党**：1866 年在美国成立的秘密组织，通过暴力重新确立了白人至上的地位。

29. **读写能力测验**：一些州和地方政府在吉姆·克劳法时期使用的测验，作为黑人投票登记程序的一部分。那些不识字或不能通过考试的人被剥夺了选举权，而黑人选举权正是宪法第十五条修正案所允许的。

30. **马克思主义**：马克思所倡导的政治制度的名称。强调掌控个人手中的生产资料，将其置于中央政府手中，从而终结资本主义。

31. **全国有色人种协进会（NAACP）**：1909 年由 W. E. B. 杜波依斯、穆尔菲尔德·斯托里和玛丽·怀特·奥文顿组建的黑人民权组织，致力于结束种族歧视，实现平等。

32. **博物学家**：研究自然史的专家，例如查尔斯·达尔文。杜波依斯出版《黑人的灵魂》时，达尔文的观点很有影响力。

33. **尼亚加拉运动**：1905 年由 W. E. B. 杜波依斯和威廉·门罗·特罗特创立的黑人民权组织。它反对布克·T. 华盛顿的妥协立场，并呼吁结束种族隔离。

34. **《物种起源》**：博物学家查尔斯·达尔文于 1859 年出版的一部开创性著作。它被公认为进化生物学的基础。在 W. E. B. 杜波依斯发表《黑人的灵魂》一书时，进化生物学认为的"黑人在生物学上不如白人"形成了当时的主流观点。

35. **泛非主义**：所有非洲血统的人都有共同的利益，应该团结起来。

36. **普莱西诉弗格森案**：1896 年美国一桩具有里程碑意义的案件，支持州和地方政府在"分离但平等"原则下实行隔离的权利。

37. **人头税**：作为投票先决条件而征收的税。在吉姆·克劳法时期，一些州和地方政府实施了一项税收，阻止了那些不能或不想缴税的黑人行使他们的选举权，而黑人选举权正是美国宪法第十五修正案所规定的。

38. **新教徒**：以宗教改革的原则为基础的基督徒。杜波依斯具有新教徒的家庭背景。

39. **重建**：1865 年至 1877 年期间，美国联邦政府将南方各州重新合并为联邦。

40. **俄国革命**：1917 年俄国发生的一系列革命，推翻了沙皇统治，促成了苏联的建立。杜波依斯研究了俄国革命，并于 1927 年前往俄国。

41. **科学方法**：一种调查方法，通过对问题的识别，然后进行观察和实验来建构解决问题的方法。杜波依斯将科学方法应用在了他的开创性著作中。

42. **苏联**：存在于 1922 年至 1991 年的社会主义联邦共和国，官方称为苏维埃社会主义共和国联盟。

43. **十中有一的人才**：杜波依斯用这个词来指代受过良好教育的精英黑人领袖，他们可以领导群众为平等而斗争。这是基于每 10 个黑人中就有 1 个能成为这样的领袖的假设。

44. **世界黑人进步协会**：1914 年成立的一个兄弟会，旨在鼓励黑人团结一致，使他们能够脱离白人社会，实行自治。

45. **死亡笼罩的幽谷**：《圣经·诗篇》23：4 中使用的一个短语。它指的是一种严重危险的情况，而如果人们不惧怕邪恶，那么希望仍然存在。杜波依斯认为，尽管黑人遭受了巨大的歧视，但他们的反抗斗争最终会使他们克服偏见。

46. **华沙犹太人区**：二战期间欧洲被占领区中最大的犹太人区。

47. **第二次世界大战**：1939—1945 年涉及世界上绝大多数国家的全球性战争，包括当时所有的强国。

人名表

1. 汉娜·阿伦特（1906—1975），20世纪最著名的政治理论家之一。她坚定地反对极权主义，支持自由，分析了不同形式的歧视之间的关系。

2. 霍米·K.巴巴（1949年生），安妮·F.罗森伯格英美文学与语言教授，哈佛大学人文中心主任。在《文化的定位》一书中，巴巴扩展了杜波依斯关于双重意识的观点，认为在后殖民时代，有一个存在于"殖民者"和"被殖民者"之间的人的第三空间。

3. 安德鲁·布林斯利，南卡罗来纳大学黑人研究领域的社会学家和著名学者。他认为《黑人的灵魂》是对黑人精神的深刻洞察，而这一点在学术文献中却被忽视了。

4. 托马斯·卡莱尔（1795—1881），苏格兰哲学家和历史学家。他在《论历史上的英雄、英雄崇拜和英雄业绩》一书中认为，伟人通过他们的天分、智慧、魅力和政治敏锐性来改变历史。

5. 奥古斯特·孔德（1798—1857），法国哲学家，社会学和实证主义学说的创始人。实证主义学说认为知识可以通过科学的检验。

6. 查尔斯·达尔文（1809—1882），英国博物学家和地质学家，被认为是进化论之父，他的理论质疑了上帝创世的观点。

7. 苏拉妮·戴维斯（1949年生），美国著名作家和剧作家。她曾在美国的剧院里对杜波依斯的作品做了戏剧朗诵。

8. 南希·丹顿，奥尔巴尼大学社会学教授，曾发表《美国种族隔离》等著作。她强调了《黑人的灵魂》对于种族主义和黑人身份的重要性，认为种族主义仍然是美国社会的一个主要问题。

9. 弗雷德里克·道格拉斯（1818—1995），曾是一名奴隶，后来成功脱逃，成为美国废奴运动的作家、演说家、政治家和领袖。

10. 约翰·F.多维迪奥，耶鲁大学心理学教授。他认为，自从W.E.

B. 杜波依斯出版了《黑人的灵魂》之后，种族主义的措词发生了变化；他声称，今天的种族主义更加微妙，并以为多元文化主义、反种族主义和平等主义的形式出现。

11. **拉尔夫·沃尔多·爱默生**（1803—1882），19 世纪美国著名作家和哲学家。他倡导超验主义，认为哲学和文学应该挑战当前社会和文化的现状。在他的作品中，他创造了"双重意识"这个词，但他没有像杜波依斯那样把这个概念与非裔美国人联系起来。

12. **弗朗茨·法农**（1925—1961），在马提尼克出生的法国黑人哲学家和革命家，著有《大地上的受苦者》和《黑皮肤，白面具》。杜波依斯影响了他对种族主义和黑人身份的研究。

13. **E. 富兰克林·弗雷泽**（1894—1962），美国社会学家和作家。他有关美国黑人的著作颇多，包括《美国黑人家庭》。他认为，W.E.B. 杜波依斯在《黑人的灵魂》中描述的乡村的种族隔离、肮脏和缺乏机会的现象，如今却发生在城市里。

14. **塞缪尔·L. 盖特纳**，特拉华大学的心理学教授。他认为，自从 W.E.B. 杜波依斯出版了《黑人的灵魂》之后，种族主义的话语发生了变化；他声称，今天的种族主义更加微妙，并以为多元文化主义、反种族主义和平等主义的形式出现。

15. **马库斯·加维**（1887—1940），牙买加政治领袖。他推动了黑人民族主义（即白人和黑人生活在不同的社会中）的事业。他是黑星星航运公司的创始人，希望使所有的非洲裔都返回非洲。

16. **保罗·吉尔罗伊**（1956 年生），伦敦国王学院的英美文学教授。吉尔罗伊在《黑大西洋》中将全球黑人遭遇种族主义的生活经历联系起来，扩展了杜波依斯的思想。

17. **尤利西斯·格兰特**（1822—1885），1869 年到 1877 年间担任美国陆军将军和总统，他领导联邦军队在内战中取得胜利，在重建期间担任总统。

18. **G. W. F. 黑格尔**（1770—1831），德国哲学家。他的理论对卡尔·马克思产生了深远的影响。在《黑人的灵魂》中，杜波依斯将黑格尔

在《精神现象学》中关于历史和意识之间的联系运用到美国的非裔美国人身上。

19. 亨利·詹姆斯（1843—1916），著名的英美作家，著有《一位女士的画像》和《螺丝在旋紧》。他对杜波依斯在《黑人的灵魂》一书中的文学才华称赞有加。

20. 拉迪亚德·吉卜林（1865—1936），出生在印度的英国作家，是19世纪和20世纪最受欢迎的作家之一。他是《白人的负担》这首诗的作者，在诗中他写道，殖民主义是一项崇高的使命，因为白人被赋予了教化黑人的责任。

21. 马丁·路德·金（1929—1968），浸礼会牧师和活动家。从20世纪50年代到1968年被暗杀，他一直领导美国的民权运动。金继承了尼亚加拉运动和全国有色人种协进会的创始人之一杜波依斯的思想遗产。

22. 大卫·利弗林·刘易斯（1936年生），纽约大学历史学教授。他的W. E. B. 杜波依斯传记二部曲获得了两项普利策奖。

23. 亚伯拉罕·林肯（1809—1865），1861年担任美国总统，1865年遇刺。他领导国家经历了内战，废除了奴隶制。

24. 埃里克·林肯（1924—2000），非裔美国学者，曾在包括杜克大学在内的美国多所大学任教。他认为《黑人的灵魂》是对黑人精神的深刻洞察，而这一点在学术文献中却被忽视了。

25. 卡尔·马克思（1818—1883），德国哲学家、经济学家、历史学家和社会学家，被公认为历史上最具影响力的社会科学家之一。虽然杜波依斯在写《黑人的灵魂》时对马克思主义只有基本的理解，但他后来的作品如《黑人的重建》反映了其对资本主义与种族主义的关系更深刻的理解。

26. 道格拉斯·梅西（1952年生），普林斯顿大学社会学教授。他强调了W. E. B. 杜波依斯作品的重要性，并在自己的作品中明确指出，种族主义仍然是美国社会的一个主要问题。

27. 赫伯特·斯宾塞（1820—1903），英国哲学家、生物学家和社会学家，是查尔斯·达尔文之前进化论领域的重要人物。他创造了"适者生存"这个词。

28. **布克·T. 华盛顿**（1856—1915），1890 年至 1915 年间美国最杰出的黑人领袖。他认为，黑人应该接受白人种族主义和政治统治，以换取基本法律权利和基本教育。而这是 W. E. B. 杜波依斯坚决反对的立场。

29. **马克斯·韦伯**（1864—1920），德国哲学家、社会学家、政治经济学家。他深刻影响了社会理论、社会研究和社会学。当杜波依斯在柏林学习时，他接触了韦伯并研究了他的思想。

30. **康奈尔·韦斯特**（1953 年生），普林斯顿大学第一位黑人哲学博士研究生，是当今美国著名的知识分子。他强调了 W. E. B. 杜波依斯作品的重要性，并问道：为什么今天很少有像杜波依斯这样的黑人？

31. **罗伯特·沃瑟姆**，北卡罗来纳中央大学的社会学教授。他认为社会学家经常忽视 W. E. B. 杜波依斯的伟大贡献。

32. **厄尔·赖特**，辛辛那提大学的非洲研究教授。他是 W. E. B. 杜波依斯研究专家。

33. **沙蒙·查米尔**，纽约大学阿布扎比分校的文学和视觉研究教授。著有《黑暗之声：W. E. B. 杜波依斯与美国思想：1888—1903》。

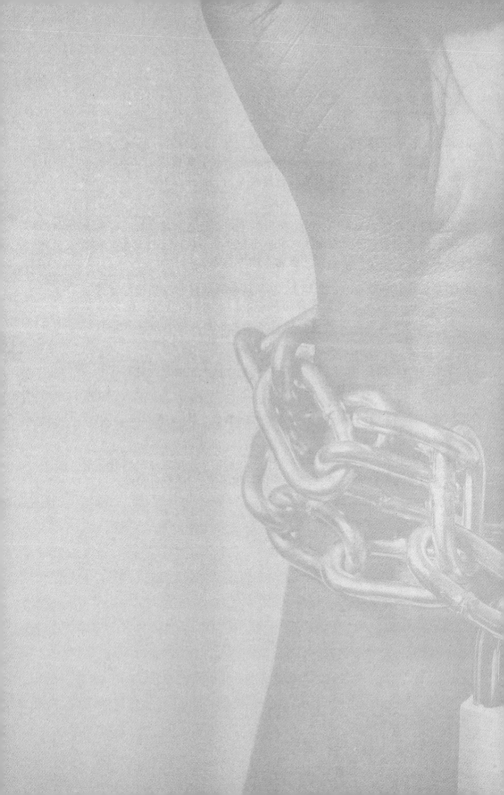

WAYS IN TO THE TEXT

- The teaching, research, journalism and activism of W. E. B. Du Bois (1868–1963) shaped the movements that ended racial segregation in the United States and colonialism in Africa and Asia.

- *The Souls of Black Folk* puts forward the idea that whites invented the concept of racism to advance their material wealth. This had serious negative consequences for black identity, democracy and humanity and could only be overcome by black pride, resistance and struggle.

- Souls went against the dominant view in early twentieth century America that blacks were biologically inferior to whites, which explained their position in society.

Who Was W. E. B. Du Bois?

William Edward Burghardt Du Bois was born in Great Barrington, Massachusetts in 1868. He excelled as a scholar and in 1895 became the first African American to earn a PhD from Harvard University. He went on to become a professor, journalist and activist, making huge contributions to society. Throughout his life he exposed the actual causes of racism in the United States and elsewhere, while explaining the effects racism had on black identity. He continually stressed the need to overcome racism to achieve genuine democracy and greater human understanding. Du Bois revived, then continued, the great legacy of Frederick Douglass,* who escaped slavery to become a prominent black intellectual. Du Bois became a central force in shaping the movements that ended racial segregation in the United States and colonialism in Africa and Asia and so can be considered one of history's great figures.

What Does *The Souls of Black Folk* Say?

W. E. B. Du Bois published *The Souls of Black Folk* in 1903. It consists of 14 essays on racism, some of which had already been published in the literary and cultural magazine, the *Atlantic Monthly*.* These essays draw from the author's personal experiences and research.

In *Souls*, Du Bois uses a range of literary techniques to describe the conditions of racism and inequality in what was known as Jim Crow* America. This long period began in 1877 and ended in the 1960s. During this era, state governments implemented a variety of measures that encouraged racism, segregation and inequality. These measures were then reinforced by national Federal legislation. All of this took place despite the fact that the Thirteenth Amendment to the American Constitution* had abolished slavery in 1865 and the Fifteenth Amendment, passed in 1870, granted blacks the right to vote.

Souls challenged the dominant academic and mainstream position at the time that claimed blacks were both biologically and culturally inferior to whites. The British naturalist* Charles Darwin* was one person who advanced this view. Du Bois opposed this claim in detail by showing how whites invented the concept of "racism" to advance their material wealth.

In *Souls* he argues that "the color line"—a metaphor he uses for racism—is and will be the greatest problem America faces in the twentieth century. In Du Bois's view, racism undermined both democracy and humanity. For America to truly be "one nation, indivisible under God," as the country so often claimed it was, whites would have to acknowledge the past and blacks would have to be equal citizens. Du Bois drew from German philosopher G. W. F. Hegel's* analysis of history and consciousness* (or the awareness of oneself) in his 1807 book *The Phenomenology of Spirit* to argue that racism prevented both white and black Americans from fulfilling their potential.

Like Frederick Douglass before him, Du Bois encouraged blacks to become educated, to become leaders, to take pride in their heritage and culture and to struggle against white oppression. This position was in contrast to the view of Booker T.Washington,* another great African American figure of the time. Washington argued that blacks should accommodate white racism in exchange for a basic education and basic legal rights.

In *Souls*, Du Bois introduces two important concepts that further develop his idea of "the color line." The first is "double consciousness," which refers to the difficulties blacks face attempting to be both African and American in a white racist society. The second is "the veil," which metaphorically refers to racism as a kind of frontier dividing blacks and whites. This weighs heavily on both black and white souls and prevents both of them from achieving their full potential.

Throughout the text Du Bois makes it clear he is optimistic that one day America will lift this "veil." He believes this will happen when whites acknowledge the injustices of the past and blacks become equal citizens. When the veil is finally lifted, America will be a true democracy, humanity in general will transcend everything else and the American soul will be at peace.

Why Does *The Souls of Black Folk* Matter?

In *Souls*, Du Bois went against accepted early twentieth-century American thinking that blacks were biologically inferior to whites, presenting an alternative to Booker T. Washington's accommodationist stance. Du Bois achieved this by suggesting the capitalist* economic system led white people to be racist, and by encouraging black struggle. The text provides real insight into what shapes discrimination, how it conditions identity and how it must be overcome. Although Du Bois focused *The Souls of Black Folk* entirely on Jim Crow America, his later work addressed racism at a global level and was in favor of the collective struggle of all oppressed minorities. Du Bois's body of work—and *Souls* in particular—has inspired activists around the world. *Souls* lies at the intersection of African American studies, critical race and ethnicity theory and postcolonial studies. The book has huge interdisciplinary value, because it has been a starting point for further scholarship in a number of fields, ranging from history to sociology and from economics to politics.

SECTION 1
INFLUENCES

THE AUTHOR AND THE
HISTORICAL CONTEXT

KEY POINTS

* *The Souls of Black Folk* is a seminal work in the field of sociology and a classic of American literature. It is one of the most important texts ever written on racism and black identity in America.

* Du Bois gained a much deeper understanding of racism in America in 1885 when he moved from Massachusetts in the north to study in Tennessee in the south.

* The Jim Crow* era was a period when state and local governments passed laws that discriminated against blacks. It started in 1877 and lasted until the civil rights movements of the 1960s.

Why Read This Text?

The Souls of Black Folk is a collection of 14 essays about racism written by American historian, sociologist and civil rights activist W. E. B. Du Bois. Published in 1903, it is one of the most important texts ever written in the field of sociology and is a classic of American literature. *Souls* is an essential read for anyone who wants to understand the many different elements that make up the history of black Americans. These include:

* Their identity and their awareness of it (consciousness)
* The discrimination and inequality they have experienced
* Links between racism and economics

- The role of education and leadership in shaping change
- The need to overcome injustice to reach a greater level of humanity

Du Bois combines social analysis, religious references, literary metaphors and scientific research (using many different methods) in his work. All this leads to a mature, in-depth analysis of racism in late nineteenth and early twentieth century America and the struggle of blacks to overcome it. Throughout *Souls* the author puts across a sense of sorrow, but also one of deep optimism. Du Bois believed that one day black resistance and struggle would overcome the Jim Crow laws that legalized segregation at state and local levels and which led to black oppression and inequality. As he prophetically puts it in the text: "Someday the Awakening will come, when the pent-up vigor of ten-million souls shall sweep irresistibly towards the Goal, out of the Valley of the Shadow of Death."[*1]

Throughout the essays, Du Bois puts across a core message. Racism is a social construction that uses race, class and gender for political and economic ends. Its aim is to categorize, humiliate and exploit black people, primarily to make money. This, he says, can be seen in his current-day reality, as well as in the history of American slavery. The author argues that only a "Great Awakening" of black pride, resistance and struggle can overcome racism. In reality, this meant blacks having not only equal legal citizenship and the right to vote, but also the same opportunities as whites in education and employment. Only in these circumstances could everyone move on from past suffering and enjoy a greater sense of common humanity for whites and blacks alike.

> *"History cannot ignore W. E. B. Du Bois because history has to reflect truth and Dr. Du Bois was a tireless explorer and a gifted discoverer of social truths. His singular greatness lay in his quest for truth about his own people. There were very few scholars who concerned themselves with honest study of the black man and he sought to fill this immense void. The degree to which he succeeded disclosed the great dimensions of the man."*
>
> ——Dr. Martin Luther King Jr.*

Author's Life

William Edward Burghardt Du Bois was born in 1868 in Great Barrington, Massachusetts. Because his mother was a descendant not only of Africans but also of English and Dutch ancestors, William was part of a very small, free, land-owning black population. His mother, Mary, worked as a domestic servant and his father, Alfred, was unemployed, which meant that money was tight. Alfred abandoned the family only a year after William was born and never returned. Mary died when William was just 17, turning him into a poor orphan.

Du Bois attended a mostly white school and worshiped at a mainly white Protestant* church. Naturally intelligent, he became the first black graduate of his high school in 1884, earning high honors. With money he saved from working and with financial help from his local church, Du Bois enrolled at Fisk University in Nashville, Tennessee. There he earned a Bachelor of Arts degree, before adding another in History from Harvard University in his native Massachusetts. His experiences at Fisk in the American south, where the Jim Crow laws were fully embraced, shaped his views on society forever. It was there that Du Bois came to deeply understand racism in America and how it affected black identity.[2]

Du Bois never felt a part of Harvard but he understood how important studying at one of America's most respected universities was for his intellectual development and reputation. He always stressed that good education was the main way for blacks to become socially mobile and to challenge oppression. Du Bois became Harvard's first African American doctoral graduate. His Ph dissertation, written in the Department of History, was entitled "The Suppression of the African Slave-Trade to the United States of America, 1638–1870." At this time he also studied at Friedrich Wilhelm University in Berlin, investigating the work of sociologists and philosophers Max Weber,* Karl Marx* and other important German scholars.[3] Influenced by socialist ideas,[4] it was around this time that Du Bois first wrote of his desire to "work for the rise of the Negro people."[5] For the rest of his life he promoted equality through his academic scholarship and teaching (at Wilberforce University, the University of Pennsylvania, and Atlanta University), as well as through his journalism and political activism.

Author's Background

Du Bois published his most important work, *The Souls of Black Folk*, in 1903 against the backdrop of the Jim Crow laws. In 1870 the American Congress* passed the Fifteenth Amendment to the country's Constitution,* granting African Americans the right to vote. Yet from 1877 and the end of Reconstruction*—the rebuilding of the country following the Civil War* of 1861–65—right through to the civil rights movement of the 1960s, white southerners put an abundance of measures in place to stop blacks from achieving equality. For example, from 1890 to 1910 new state constitutions and laws imposed taxes and literacy tests* that were deliberately designed to stop blacks from voting, even though they already had that right by law. Anyone who could not pay the taxes that were suddenly part of voting registration or could not read was not allowed to vote. White intimidation of blacks also hindered progress.

The 1896 Supreme Court case *Plessy versus Ferguson*,* meanwhile, established that the federal government could not intervene to prevent states from imposing local segregation laws in many important areas, including employment, housing and public transportation.[6]

When Du Bois decided to leave Massachusetts in 1885 and attend Fisk University in Tennessee he understood that he would gain a much deeper understanding of racism in America. As he put it,"I was going into the South; the South of slavery, rebellion and black folk; above all, I was going to meet colored people of my own age and education, of my own ambition."[7]

At Fisk, Du Bois quickly noticed that white southerners were bitter over their defeat in the Civil War—where the southern states had failed to break away from the existing Union—and the abolition of slavery in 1865. Furthermore, he witnessed blacks suffering from extreme poverty, lack of opportunity and violence. As he put it, "No one but a Negro going into the South without previous experience of color caste can have any conception of its barbarism ... I only sensed scorn and hate; the kind of despising which a dog might incur ... Murder, killing and maiming Negroes, raping Negro women ... this was not even news; it got no publicity, it caused no arrest."[8]

It was this historical backdrop of Jim Crow racism coupled with Du Bois's own experiences living in the American north and south—and Europe as well—that pushed him to become an intellectual leader of the Negro cause and of blacks everywhere. Du Bois's passion for justice lasted from the last decade of the nineteenth century until his death in newly-independent Ghana in 1963 at the grand age of 95.

1. W. E. B. Du Bois, *The Souls of Black Folk* (New York and London: W.W. Norton and Company, 1999), xxxi.

2. Du Bois, *The Souls of Black Folk*, xiii–xv.

3. Du Bois, *The Souls of Black Folk*, xvi–xix.

4. Zhang Juguo, *W. E. B. Du Bois: The Question for the Abolition of the Color Line* (New York: Routledge, 2001), 135.

5. Du Bois, *The Souls of Black Folk*, xvii, xviii.

6. J. Morgan Kousser, *The Shaping of Southern Politics: Suffrage, Restrictions and the Establishment of the One-Party South*, 1880–1910 (New Haven: Yale University Press, 1974).

7. Du Bois, *The Souls of Black Folk*, 1999, xxv.

8. Du Bois, *The Souls of Black Folk*, 1999, xxv.

ACADEMIC CONTEXT

KEY POINTS

* Du Bois argued that whites socially constructed—or invented the concept of—"race" to advance their own interests. This argument challenged the dominant view that blacks were biologically and culturally inferior to whites.

* Du Bois was inspired by the struggles of Frederick Douglass who escaped slavery and became a notable black intellectual leader in the nineteenth century.

* Du Bois adapted German philosopher G. W. F. Hegel's* understanding of the relationship between history and consciousness* to the study of racism in America and the divided consciousness of African Americans.

The Work in Its Context

Sociology—the scientific study of social behavior—is a relatively modern idea dating back to the late eighteenth century. The discipline developed as a response to advances in science, a decline in the influence of religion, industrialization and urbanization (the shift of population from rural to urban areas).

When W. E. B. Du Bois published *The Souls of Black Folk* in 1903 most sociologists believed that human progress occurred as our species evolved at a biological level. Herbert Spencer,* an early English sociologist of the mid-nineteenth century, was a champion of this view. His views were closely associated with those of the famous English naturalist* Charles Darwin,* who published *On the*

*Origin of Species** (1859) and *The Descent of Man* (1871). Darwin argued that the "white and black races" differed from each other in intellectual capability.[1]

These ideas developed out of the Enlightenment* movement of the late eighteenth century which looked to human reason and science for answers. In America, arguments in favor of evolutionary biology* like Spencer's highlighted the "stalled development" and "primitive nature" of black people. European colonial powers were quick to justify their expansion into Africa and Asia and their exploitation of these countries by spreading the idea that they were naturally superior to the native people who lived there. They claimed that, in fact, it was their *duty* to guide these people towards a "higher state of being." This idea is sometimes referred to as "the White Man's Burden"[2] after a poem of the same name by the Englishman Rudyard Kipling.* This expansion into other territories was also called the civilizing mission.*

Rapid industrialization and urbanization took place in America after the Civil War* as huge numbers of people—many of them black—flocked to cities in search of work. Academics started to use the scientific method* to study social conditions in the United States. This approach involves posing a question and predicting what the answer may be, then carrying out tests and experiments to prove whether that answer is true or false. Several universities began offering PhD programs in sociology and in 1895 W. E. B. Du Bois became the first African American to receive a doctorate from Harvard.

The Souls of Black Folk made a groundbreaking contribution to the field of sociology by challenging the dominant set of beliefs that white people were racially superior. The book argued that white elites in the United States deliberately created a society in which racism was rife and that inequality was a direct result of capitalism* and the country's history of black slavery. These two factors made it extremely difficult for black people to progress.

> "The white man's happiness cannot be purchased by the black man's misery. Virtue cannot prevail among the white people, by its destruction among the black people... It is evident that white and black 'must fall or flourish together.'"
>
> ——Frederick Douglass,* *Frederick Douglass: Selected Speechings and Writings*

Overview of the Field

French philosopher Auguste Comte* is widely regarded as a founding father of sociology[3] and his work *A General View of Positivism* (1848) first introduced the idea of using the scientific method of the natural sciences to study the structure of society.

Inspired by rational, science-based Enlightenment* thought, he argued that social evolution consisted of three phases. The first was theological, asserting that religion determined one's position in society. In other words, everyone had a "God-given" place on the social ladder. The King, for example, was at the top of the ladder because of his alleged unique relationship with God.

The second phase was metaphysical, a period during which rational scientific thought challenged the "God-given" phase by promoting a respect for universal rights and human progress. The French Revolution* of 1789 and *The Declaration of the Rights of Man and of the Citizen** are examples of this.

The final phase was positivist, which meant actively applying the scientific method to the study of problems such as inequality, rather than merely accepting philosophies of natural rights and equalities put forward in works such as *The Declaration of the Rights of Man*.

Like Comte, German revolutionary socialist Karl Marx* applied the scientific method to understanding social change and progress. From the 1840s onwards he argued that history was a product of the struggle between the ruling class and the working class. He believed that workers would eventually unite to overthrow both the ruling class and capitalism itself and replace it with a communist* society free of exploitation. There are obvious parallels between Marx's view and Du Bois's argument that racism in the United States was based on economics, though it is worth noting that, at the time Du Bois was writing *Souls*, Marx's influence in American academia was limited.[4]

Academic Influences

American writer Ralph Waldo Emerson* coined the term "double consciousness" in his book *The Transcendentalist*, written in 1843. Du Bois extended this idea by applying the term to the social psychology of "race relations." He used it to explain the psychological state of having both an African heritage and either a European or American "upbringing" under slavery. Du Bois described this double consciousness as seeing your own life through other people's eyes.

At Harvard, Du Bois studied German philosophy and, in writing *Souls*, he drew on G. W. F. Hegel's *The Phenomenology of Spirit*. Professor of Literature Shamoon Zamir* has argued that Hegel gave Du Bois the means to theorize "the relationship of consciousness to history."[5]

In *Phenomenology*, Hegel used the example of the master and the slave to show how unequal power relations lead to a lack of recognition of the individual. This in turn obstructs a person's self-consciousness, or their knowledge of themselves as a person. It is necessary to be recognized as an autonomous (self-governing) individual by others in order to be free and self-realized (able to fulfill one's own potential). If there is no such recognition, the master defines the slave's identity and the slave's consciousness of himself as an individual is damaged, which results in the slave existing in an oppressed state.

Du Bois applies Hegel's concept to "post-emancipation America" (the period after slavery was abolished), arguing that white racism had serious consequences for black identity. African Americans had made significant gains during the period of Reconstruction following the end of the Civil War in 1865. These included the abolition* of slavery, the prohibition of racial discrimination and the granting of citizenship and the right to vote. Despite this, Du Bois shows how the same power relations that existed under slavery had been reproduced by Jim Crow* laws which helped create discrimination in what was called a "separate but equal" society. This led as a result to a form of reenslavement, with states prohibiting inter-ethnic marriages, imposing segregation between races and creating literacy tests* and poll taxes* specifically to prevent blacks from voting.

This re-enslavement, Du Bois argued, created a divided consciousness inside the mind of African Americans that could only be overcome by social conflict and an eventual white recognition of equality.

Finally, the work of Scottish philosopher Thomas Carlyle* influenced Du Bois's desire to be a leader of the black cause.[6] Carlyle advanced the Great Man Theory,* which argued that great men used their intelligence, wisdom, charisma and political acumen to make history. In this sense Du Bois hoped to succeed Frederick Douglass, the escaped slave who had become a black leader through scholarship, in guiding black resistance and struggle.

---

1. Charles Darwin, *The Descent of Man* (London: John Murray, 1871), 216–7.

2. Rudyard Kipling, "The White Man's Burden," *McClure's Magazine* 12 (1899): 290–1.

3. See, for example, the back cover of: Auguste Comte, *Comte: Early Political Writings,* ed. H.S. Jones (Cambridge: Cambridge University Press, 1998).

4. There is a long-standing debate why the United States has never had a socialist influence/labor movement comparable to some European countries. This dates back to Alexis de Tocqueville's idea of "American exceptionalism." See, for example: Seymour Martin Lipsct and Gary Marks, *It Didn't Happen Here: Why Socialism Failed in America* (New York: W.W. Norton & Company, 2001).

5. Shamoon Zamir, *W. E. B. Du Bois and American Thought: 1888–1903* (Chicago: University of Chicago, 1995), 117.

6. For further details, see: Zhang Juguo, *W. E. B. Du Bois: The Question for the Abolition of the Color Line* (New York: Routledge, 2001), *W. E. B.* 29.

THE PROBLEM

KEY POINTS

* The key question among black intellectuals at the time of publication of *The Souls of Black Folk* was: how can African Americans best advance their position in racist America?

* In 1895 Booker T. Washington,* a prominent black intellectual of the era, agreed with white southerners that blacks would accept white political rule in exchange for a basic education and basic legal rights, a settlement known as the Atlanta Compromise.*

* Du Bois argued that blacks should not make compromises and should struggle against white racism to achieve equality.

Core Question

The Souls of Black Folk addresses three core questions:

* Why do whites continue to oppress African Americans even after the Civil War* and Reconstruction*?

* How does racism affect African American identity?

* How can African Americans climb the social ladder in a racist society?

W. E. B. Du Bois responds to these questions with a combination of sorrow, suffering and hope.

For Du Bois, Frederick Douglass* had been "the greatest of American Negro leaders."[1] Douglass escaped from slavery and became a social reformer, public speaker and influential writer. He led the abolitionist movement* to end slavery and played a key role in shaping President Abraham Lincoln's* Emancipation Proclamation* of 1863, which stated that all slaves in the rebellious southern states would be free. During the course of his lifetime Douglass wrote three autobiographies in which he described profound racism in America and called for black struggle.

Du Bois was deeply affected by Douglass's death, so much so that he expressed his innermost feelings in a series of elegies* entitled *The Passing of Douglass*. Du Bois tried to revive and continue his legacy by becoming the new intellectual leader of the African American cause. He successfully continued Douglass's work by defending the view that racism was a white political-economic tool to exploit black labor.

> "There can be no doubt of Mr. Washington's mistakes and shortcomings: he never adequately grasped the growing bond of politics and industry ... In stern justice, we must lay on the soul of this man, a heavy responsibility for the consummation of Negro disenfranchisement, the decline of the Negro college and public school and the firmer establishment of color caste in this land."
>
> ——W. E. B. Du Bois, *The Souls of Black Folk*

The Participants

In 1845, Frederick Douglass published his first autobiography, *The Narrative of the Life of Frederick Douglass*. The text traces the life of the author and his escape from slavery, focusing on the masters' brutal domination of slaves and his own experience of being worked to complete exhaustion and whipped when he could work no longer. The text played an important role in the abolitionist movement of the mid-nineteenth century in the United States. It sold thousands of copies[2] when it was published and challenged the dominant white view that blacks were unintelligent and incapable of producing intellectual work. Douglass went on to publish two more autobiographies, *My Bondage and My Freedom* (1855) and *The Life and Times of Frederick Douglass* (1881).

Du Bois believed that Douglass had been the greatest of role models for blacks and was concerned that, after his death, Booker T. Washington had become the dominant figure in the African American community. Du Bois did not believe Washington represented the community's interests. In 1895, Washington criticized blacks for seeking political and economic power during Reconstruction and struck an agreement with white southerners called the Atlanta Compromise, which declared that southern blacks would submit to white political rule in exchange for a basic education and basic legal rights.

The Contemporary Debate

Washington argued that blacks should get over the injustices of the past, accept discrimination, undertake industrial education intended to get them into jobs, integrate into the dominant society and prove to whites through hard work and by being good consumers that they were worthy of better treatment. Under the Atlanta Compromise, blacks would not rise up against racism and would not demand the right to vote.

Du Bois strongly disagreed with Washington's stance, claiming that blacks would only perpetuate white oppression if they accepted this relationship. Du Bois's alternative proposed that blacks should resist all domination and wage a struggle for civic equality, the right to vote, equal education and the establishment of a true meritocracy in which individuals would be judged on their abilities, not on their race.

The Souls of Black Folk gave voice to a developing black collective consciousness (a sense of themselves as a group) and a shared black culture. This came at a time when former slaves and the children of slaves were struggling to gain a sense of who they were and what their community represented in the aftermath of the Civil War and Reconstruction. Du Bois was the leader of their resistance to white rule and the struggle born from the chaos of slavery. He also galvanized opposition to the Jim Crow laws at a time when clear attempts were being made to make African Americans officially inferior in civil terms, through segregation and by withdrawing aid from black educational institutions.

For these reasons, *Souls* was a highly significant response to the dominant position of whites and to the stance of Booker T. Washington, who was willing to work within the system to improve things for blacks. It provided an alternative view of racism in America and addressed how blacks should respond to it. But it also set out intellectual arguments for the way to achieve black progress and develop a black middle class.

---

1. Du Bois, *The Souls of Black Folk*, xii.
2. Frederick Douglass, introduction to *Narrative of the Life of Frederick Douglass: An American Slave*, ed. Benjamin Quarles (Cambridge, MA: Harvard University Press, 1988).

MODULE 4

THE AUTHOR'S CONTRIBUTION

KEY POINTS

* The ideas contained in *The Souls of Black Folk* revive the beliefs of former slave and black intellectual Frederick Douglass* and serve as an inspiration for blacks in America and elsewhere. They oppose the accommodationist stance of Booker T. Washington.*

* The book challenges the dominant view in academia and politics that blacks were biologically and culturally inferior to whites.

* Du Bois argues that racism in his country is an invented concept rooted in capitalism* and America's legacy of slavery. He believes that black resistance, pride, and struggle will eventually overcome prejudice.

Author's Aims

W. E. B. Du Bois's *The Souls of Black Folk* revived the legacy of former slave Frederick Douglass and put it back on the political agenda. Douglass had led the movement to abolish slavery in the United States and gained fame among blacks as a charismatic and persuasive writer and public speaker. He fought for universal equality, challenging the dominant white view that blacks were not intelligent enough to be intellectuals. His autobiographies depicted the horrors of slavery, but his escape and rise to prominence proved an inspiration to many.

After Douglass's death in 1895, Booker T. Washington

became one of the most recognized black intellectuals in America. His view was that blacks should in the short term submit to racism and white political rule in exchange for basic concessions. By means of scholarship, journalism and activism, Du Bois challenged the view that blacks were biologically inferior to whites by showing how white capitalist greed depended on slavery and racism to make money from cheap labor. This position was revolutionary at the time and met with mixed reactions.[1] Unlike Washington, who believed that blacks should accept being "second-class citizens," Du Bois argued that whites and blacks could overcome the injustice of the past and create a humane society grounded in equality.

> "Dr. Du Bois was not only an intellectual giant exploring the frontiers of knowledge, he was in the first place a teacher ... One idea he insistently taught was that black people have been kept in oppression and deprivation by a poisonous fog of lies that depicted them as inferior, born deficient and deservedly doomed to servitude to the grave ... The twisted logic ran if the black man was inferior he was not oppressed—his place in society was appropriate to his meager talent and intellect."
>
> —— Dr. Martin Luther King Jr.

Approach

In line with developments in sociology and the social sciences, Du Bois applied the scientific method* (working out answers to problems through experiments and the use of hard data) to understanding social problems—in this case racism and inequality—and their effects on African American identity.

Published in 1903, *The Souls of Black Folk* built on another seminal work by Du Bois, *The Philadelphia Negro*, which had appeared four years earlier. One of the earliest examples of sociology as a statistical science, the book combines more than 5,000 interviews with ordinary people together with census data[2] to present a vivid picture of the social and economic deprivation of African Americans living in Philadelphia, Pennsylvania.

Souls opened eyes because it confronted "the scientifically proven" position that inferior biological characteristics made black people incapable of achieving equality. Du Bois explained how whites had built a society in which they were seen as intellectually and morally superior by using the concept of "race differences" to exploit blacks in order to make money for themselves. He argued that, as a result, whites were imprisoned in their own self-denial. Du Bois explained this set-up more clearly in his later work *Black Reconstruction*: "Out of the exploitation of the dark proletariat [black workers] comes the Surplus Value [profit] filched from human beasts ... The emancipation of man is the emancipation of labor and the emancipation of labor is the freeing of that basic majority of workers who are yellow, brown and black."[3]

Contribution in Context

Du Bois's analysis of racism in America built on the legacy of the abolitionist movement,* which was led by former slaves such as Frederick Douglass. Du Bois's renewed call for social struggle was a continuation of this earlier ideology but his approach was more scientific, incorporating the latest developments in the social sciences to make the link between economics and racism and inequality.

Although Du Bois drew from previous scholarship by the German philosopher G. W. F. Hegel,* among others, he addressed African American identity in a new way. He applied Hegel's link between history and consciousness—as well as psychological research on split personalities—to the condition of blacks in America. He showed how their identity issues and their inability to climb the social ladder was caused by white racism insisting that social conflict, rather than accommodation (or simply accepting racist behavior), was the best approach to overcoming oppression and inequality. By stressing education, pride and leadership, Du Bois also encouraged blacks to help American society become more humane.

It is tempting to draw parallels between Du Bois's interpretation of black exploitation based on white financial gain in America and the views of German philosopher Karl Marx.* Marx took the view that history is marked by the struggle between the workers and the ruling class. However, Du Bois made it clear that at this point in his academic career he had only a rudimentary understanding of Marxism.* As he put it,"[In my early work] there are some approaches, some allusions, but no complete realization of the application of the philosophy of Karl Marx to my subject. That concept came much later, when I began intensive study of the facts of society, culminating in my *Black Reconstruction* [1935]."[4]

1. See: W. E. B. Du Bois, *The Souls of Black Folk* (New York and London: W.W. Norton and Company, 1999), 221–346.

2. See, for example, Greg Johnson, "W. E. B. Du Bois' The Philadelphia Negro," *Penn Current*, July 2, 2009, accessed January 20, 2015, http://www.upenn.edu/pennnews/current/node/3997.

3. W. E. B. Du Bois, *Black Reconstruction in America* (New York: Russell and Russell, 1963), 16.

4. W. E. B. Du Bois, *The Suppression of the African Slave Trade in the United States of America, 1638–1870* (New York: The Social Science Press, 1954), 327–9.

SECTION 2
IDEAS

MAIN IDEAS

KEY POINTS

* Du Bois presents three core concepts in *Souls*: "the color line" (racism)—the main problem which confronts America in the twentieth century; "double consciousness"—the psychological challenge facing blacks as they attempt to be both African and American in a racist society; "the veil"—a metaphor referring to the barrier that racism creates between whites and blacks.

* The author's hope is that one day American society will transcend its racism, that democracy will be achieved and that all of humanity will be united.

* Du Bois feels both sorrow and pain at the racism he experiences and witnesses, but is still optimistic that a more just society will emerge.

Key Themes

In the foreword ("The Forethought") of *The Souls of Black Folk*, W. E. B. Du Bois states: "Herein lie buried many things which if read with patience may show the strange meaning of being black here in the dawning of the Twentieth Century. This meaning is not without interest to you, Gentle Reader; for the problem of the Twentieth Century is the problem of the color line."[1]

This description depicts racism as *the problem* in American society, and one that has long affected black and white people alike. This is the key theme that underpins the entire book. Du Bois then reflects on how this affects the way African Americans think about the society they live in and asks the question:"How does it feel to be a problem?"[2]

The author then answers: "To be a poor man is hard, but to be a poor race in a land of dollars is the very bottom of hardships."[3]

Du Bois then discusses the legacy of the Civil War,* the Emancipation Proclamation,* the period of Reconstruction* and segregation and inequality implemented by the Jim Crow* laws. At this point he stresses the strong link between racism and capitalism.

Du Bois describes how slavery and the Jim Crow laws create a deeply engrained condition in the minds of African Americans. It is at this point that he introduces the two most important concepts of the text: double consciousness and the metaphor of the veil.

The author is also optimistic about the struggle against oppression. He emphasizes the importance of black leadership and—in contrast to another prominent black political figure, Booker T.Washington*—he argues that African Americans must engage in a social struggle which he hopes will one day bring about civic equality, the right to vote, equal education and the establishment of a meritocracy in which people are judged on their abilities alone.

> "The Nation has not yet found peace from its sins; the freedman has not yet found in freedom his promised land. Whatever of good may have come in these years of change, the shadow of a deep disappointment rests upon the Negro people."
>
> ——W. E. B. Du Bois, *The Souls of Black Folk*

Exploring the Ideas

The term "double consciousness" describes the fractured mental state of African Americans. This state is created by the daily challenge blacks face as they attempt to assimilate into a dominant white culture, while simultaneously trying to maintain a sense of pride in their own black heritage and identity. Du Bois depicts this condition as follows: "One ever feels his two-ness, an American, a Negro; two souls, two thoughts, two unreconciled strivings: two warring ideals in one dark body, whose dogged strength alone keeps it from being torn asunder."[4]

Du Bois then introduces his metaphor of "the veil," which represents the division between two worlds: a dominant white one and a politically, economically, and socially marginalized black one. The African American is constantly prevented from fulfilling his or her potential by a white, racist outlook that not only distorts reality but causes psychological torment to the black individual. As Du Bois puts it:"The Negro is ... born with a veil, and gifted with second-sight in this American world, a world which yields him no true self-consciousness, but only lets him see himself through the revelation of the other world ... This double-consciousness, this sense of always looking at one's self through the eyes of others, of measuring one's soul by the tape of a world that looks on in amused contempt and pity."[5]

In addressing this double consciousness, Du Bois talks about his own experience as a black man in this white world, describing how he was "... shut out from their world by a vast veil."[6] He illustrates his point with a story from his time at Fisk University when he gave a greeting card to a white girl who refused it on the grounds that he was a black man.

Du Bois describes three different ways that blacks react to this condition of double consciousness. They glorify their blackness to feel pride in themselves (the "Black is Beautiful"* movement of the 1960s is a good example). They seek revenge by revolting against the dominant society (as in the Black Power* movement, also in the 1960s). Or they try to adapt their behavior to white culture by assimilating into it.

Du Bois's hope is that through black pride, education, leadership and struggle blacks will transcend the veil and overcome the traumatic condition of double consciousness.

Language and Expression

Du Bois uses a variety of literary techniques, including metaphor, autobiography, Negro spirituals, biblical allusions and Greek mythology to persuade two distinct audiences of his case. The first of these is the dominant white society that stands on the other side of the veil and uses racism to marginalize African Americans. He talks about the injustices blacks suffer and calls for whites to reflect and show greater humanity. The second audience is the black society that stands behind the veil, is oppressed by the Jim Crow laws and seeks liberation from white domination. In a world of racism and inequality Du Bois hopes to lead and inspire the black reader by using a prophetic voice that highlights the rich history of African American culture, spirituality and struggle.

In addition to this range of literary techniques, Du Bois applies the scientific method* to his argument by linking sociology to economics. In particular, he emphasizes the relationship between white greed in a capitalist society and the racism and inequality suffered by the blacks who do the work.

The concepts of the "color line,""double consciousness," and "the veil" remain important to this day in the field of sociology and beyond.

---

1. Du Bois, *The Souls of Black Folk*, 5.
2. Du Bois, *The Souls of Black Folk*, 9.
3. Du Bois, *The Souls of Black Folk*, 14.
4. Du Bois, *The Souls of Black Folk*, 11.
5. Du Bois, *The Souls of Black Folk*, 10–11.
6. Du Bois, *The Souls of Black Folk*, 10.

MODULE 6
SECONDARY IDEAS

KEY POINTS

* Du Bois addresses two secondary themes in the text. First, progress towards greater equality during the Reconstruction* period has been undermined by white bitterness over both the Civil War* and the abolition of slavery. Second, religion and the black church were great sources of inspiration for black pride, resistance, and struggle during the period of the Jim Crow* laws.

* Efforts to help freed slaves to integrate into white society such as the Freedmen's Bureau* were often undermined by resentful white people.

* Religion and the black Church provided refuge for blacks in a society that oppressed them and served as a source of inspiration for collective resistance to racism.

Other Ideas

W. E. B. Du Bois's *The Souls of Black Folk* is a collection of 14 essays written over seven years, so it naturally addresses a number of secondary themes. Two of the most important are contained in "On the Dawn of Freedom" and "Of the Faith of Our Fathers."

In "On the Dawn of Freedom" Du Bois explores the Freedmen's Bureau, a federal government agency that helped freed slaves integrate into white society during the era of Reconstruction between 1865 and 1877. It was set up by President Abraham Lincoln* in 1865 and provided educational services, legal help and employment to help blacks integrate. However, its efforts were largely undermined by white southerners (such as the violent supremacist group the Ku Klux Klan*) who were bitter over the loss of the Civil War and the abolition of slavery. The establishment of the Black Codes*— laws passed by southern states in 1865 and 1866 to continue white supremacy—also hindered the Bureau. Under these codes, the presence of any amount of black blood in a person's lineage made them legally black. Public facilities were segregated meaning, for example, that a black person could not use a bathroom intended for white people. Freedmen were obliged to work but they could not be taught to read and write and were not allowed to assemble without a white person being present. These codes were designed to make sure whites had a steady supply of cheap labor. They included vagrancy statutes, which permitted whites to arrest anyone they suspected of leaving their workplace; any black person who could not pay a fine would be sentenced to forced labor. In 1872, Ulysses Grant* became president and abruptly closed the Freedmen's Bureau because of southern opposition to help being given to blacks hoping to get on in life.

The essay "Of the Faith of our Fathers" describes the history and influence of the black Church in America and how religion had shaped, and was still shaping, African American culture and resistance. Du Bois focuses in particular on the important role black preachers, either former slaves or children of slaves, played in promoting solidarity in the black community.

"To be a poor man is hard, but to be a poor race in a land of dollars is the very bottom of hardships."

——W. E. B. Du Bois, *The Souls of Black Folk*

Exploring the Ideas

In his essay "On the Dawn of Freedom," Du Bois makes one main argument: that despite claims that the Civil War began over issues of how much power each individual state should have compared to the Union, this was not the underlying cause of the war. For Du Bois, the real issue was that of slavery. "We knew that the question of Negro Slavery was the real cause of the conflict,"[1] he says.

In analyzing Reconstruction Du Bois argues that, although the Freedmen's Bureau was an important initiative, it was often undermined. While it helped freed slaves receive an education, granting them access to newly-established black schools like Fisk University, corrupt officials would often find ways to strip successful blacks of their property. As he explains, "in a distracted land where slavery had hardly fallen, to keep the strong from wanton abuse of the weak, and the weak from gloating insolently over the half-shorn strength of the strong, was a thankless, hopeless task."[2] Du Bois argues that, despite the abolition of slavery, the Jim Crow laws and other forms of racism in effect led to the re-enslavement of blacks.

In "Of the Faith of Our Fathers," Du Bois highlights the importance of religion as a uniting force among African Americans. He emphasizes the role preachers play in providing leadership in the struggle to overcome "the color line," using black faith and solidarity to transcend "the veil" and move towards liberty and justice.

Overlooked

Du Bois's work has had an enduring impact on race and ethnicity studies, as well as on post-colonial scholarship, which analyzes the material and cultural legacies of European colonialism. However, as scholars like Professor Robert Wortham* and Professor Earl Wright* have pointed out, sociologists often overlook Du Bois's influence.[3] His use of the scientific method* in the study of the condition of blacks in a political-economic context was ahead of its time, while his view of American society flew in the face of contemporary opinion which held that the position of blacks was due to "their inferior biological characteristics." These contributions put Du Bois among the most prominent sociologists of all time.

Post-colonial scholars such as Paul Gilroy* and Homi K. Bhabha* have brought back to the fore the subject of how the unequal relationship between blacks and whites conditioned identity. Gilroy has showcased how Du Bois's message linked the experiences of blacks, not just in America, but globally. As Du Bois said himself: "Peoples of the World, we American Negroes appeal to you; our treatment in America is not merely an internal question of the United States. It is a basic problem of humanity; of democracy; of discrimination because of race and color; and as such it demands your attention and action. No nation is so great that the world can afford to let it continue to be deliberately unjust, cruel, and unfair towards its own citizens."[4]

---

1. Du Bois, *The Souls of Black Folk*, 17.

2. Du Bois, *The Souls of Black Folk*, 29–30.

3. Robert A. Wortham, "Introduction to the Sociology of W. E. B. Du Bois," *Sociation Today* 3 (2005): 1; Earl Wright, "W. E. B. Du Bois and the Atlanta Sociological Laboratory," *Sociation Today* 3 (2005): 1.

4. Excerpt from W. E. B. Du Bois, *An Appeal to the World: A Statement of Denial of Human Rights to Minorities in the Case of Citizens of Negro Descent in the United States of America and an Appeal to the United Nations for Redress* (New York: National Association for the Advancement of Colored People, 1947).

ACHIEVEMENT

KEY POINTS

* W. E. B. Du Bois challenged the dominant view in American society that racism existed because blacks were biologically inferior. He did this by showing how capitalism* used the idea of supposed black racial inferiority to justify cheap labor. This view inspired black struggles across the world.

* Du Bois did not agree with the more militant stance of Marcus Garvey,* who called on black Americans to abandon their country and return to their ancestral homeland.

* Du Bois saw huge advances in the black struggle during his lifetime, but his hope for human harmony has not been fully realized because racism still exists.

Assessing the Argument

As an academic researcher, teacher, journalist and activist, W. E. B. Du Bois encouraged black struggle on a global scale by highlighting the connection between capitalist greed and racism in the United States and beyond. He encouraged blacks to fight for equality and not to accept white political rule and discrimination in exchange for a few basic concessions. The three most important concepts in *The Souls of Black Folk*—the color line, double consciousness and the veil—continue to have an important influence on race and ethnicity studies and post-colonial studies.

Despite widespread racism in American society in 1903, *Souls* made an immediate impact. Only two months after publication it was in its third printing. Although the author had already published two books and numerous scholarly and journalistic articles, this was the text that brought him international recognition. Important figures such as writer and literary critic Henry James* praised the book for its literary and social value. At the same time, many prominent southerners including another black leader, Booker T. Washington,* criticized Du Bois for stirring up "unnecessary" controversy.[1] Between 1903 and 1940 the text sold in the region of 20,000 copies. In 1953 the Blue Heron Press of New York published 1,000 copies of a 50-year commemoration edition, for which Du Bois supplied a new foreword. In 2003 commemoration events took place throughout the United States and elsewhere in appreciation of the author's legacy.[2] Despite all this, Du Bois's full intent has not been realized because racism and inequality still exist.

> "He [Du Bois] symbolized in his being his pride in the black man. He did not apologize for being black and, because of it, handicapped. Instead he attacked the oppressor for the crime of stunting black men. He confronted the establishment as a model of militant manhood and integrity. He defied them and, though they heaped venom and scorn on him, his powerful voice was never stilled."
>
> ——Dr. Martin Luther King Jr.

Achievement in Context

Building on the scholarship and activism of former slave Frederick Douglass,* Du Bois challenged white supremacy and Booker T.

Washington's position that blacks should accept discrimination in exchange for modest advances in society. Yet he also opposed the more militant stance of Marcus Garvey.

Garvey was a Jamaican-born black nationalist* who founded the Universal Negro Improvement Association* in 1914. He subsequently moved to Harlem, New York, where he argued for black purity and separation from white society, calling on all black Americans to "return" to their ancestral homeland, Africa. Although Du Bois commended Garvey for promoting black pride and confidence, he strongly disagreed with his views. Du Bois maintained that blacks were both African and American, and that neither aspect should at any point be lost. He believed that blacks could achieve equality in American society, while preserving the richness of their heritage and cultural identity, if they were properly led by an intellectual elite, or as he called it a "Talented Tenth."* Du Bois used the term to describe his original idea that one in 10 black men could become leaders and help their black fellow-men rise up. Du Bois thought that the process of black struggle and white recognition of black identity was required to cleanse the soul of both the oppressor and the oppressed, and to reach a higher state of humanity.

Souls has served as a foundation for a better understanding of racism and black identity and has provided inspiration for future black leaders and for liberation struggles, both in the United States and in former European colonies.

Although *Souls* argued for equal civil and political rights for blacks, as well as equal education and the establishment of a meritocracy, its aims have not been entirely fulfilled since publication in 1903. The author should, nevertheless, be remembered as one of the foremost sociologists in history and as someone who played an instrumental role in advancing the position of all the oppressed peoples of the world.

Limitations

The Souls of Black Folk applies first and foremost to racism and identity in the United States in the late nineteenth and early twentieth centuries. The text depicts a society that functions on white privilege and a dominant belief in white racial supremacy. As a result, blacks are second-class citizens. The 14 essays Du Bois wrote dealt with the Civil War,* slavery, Reconstruction,* the link between capitalism* and racism, the effects of racism on African American identity, religion and the black Church, pride, resistance, and struggle. The text also has a broader relevance, highlighting the ways in which whites in a capitalist society oppress ethnic minorities and how this holds back the whole of society, preventing democracy from functioning. *Souls* should be regarded as an interdisciplinary masterpiece relevant to more than one academic area of study and a text that has had considerable relevance over time.

---

1. W. E. B. Du Bois, *The Souls of Black Folk* (New York and London: W. W. Norton and Company, 1999), 221–346.
2. University of Massachusetts Libraries, Special Collections, University Archives, DuBoisopedia, December 18, 2013, accessed January 20, 2015, http://scua.library.umass.edu/duboisopedia/doku. php?id= about:souls_of_black_folk.

PLACE IN THE AUTHOR'S WORK

KEY POINTS

* W. E. B. Du Bois's body of work was all about exposing racism and highlighting its effects on identity, consciousness, democracy and humanity, then encouraging a collective struggle to overcome it.

* *The Souls of Black Folk* was one of many significant elements in Du Bois's lifelong commitment to achieving greater human understanding.

* *Souls* built on a previous work, *The Philadelphia Negro,* and gave Du Bois international recognition. His struggle against oppression then took on a global perspective.

Positioning

In 1896 W. E. B. Du Bois was hired by the University of Pennsylvania, where he began studying the living conditions of blacks in Philadelphia. This research was very advanced for its time, incorporating several different methods including interviews, participant observation and historical and data analysis. As Du Bois's biographer Professor David Levering Lewis* explains,"As he tabulated some 15,000 household schedules, he had before him life histories of the entire black population of the Seventh Ward, nearly 10,000 men, women, and children."[1]

This intensive research culminated in Du Bois's first seminal work, *The Philadelphia Negro*, which he published while working at Atlanta University in 1899. In 1903 Du Bois went on to publish

The Souls of Black Folk, which again employed mixed research methods and further highlighted the conditions of racism and inequality in America. This was a mature work, establishing the author as a serious national and international scholar.

True to his lifelong-held philosophy that researchers should apply their science to bring about social change, Du Bois left Atlanta University in 1910 to lead the National Association for the Advancement of Colored Peoples (NAACP).*

In 1920, he published *Darkwater:Voices from within the Veil,* the first of his three autobiographies. This dealt with the oppression of blacks globally and included a chapter on the resistance and struggles of black women in particular. By now, Du Bois's vision was pan-African,* universal even, encouraging minority struggles against oppression everywhere.

Black Reconstruction in America followed in 1935, looking at different economic classes during the period of Reconstruction.* It argued that the failure of white and black workers to unite against oppressive white property owners allowed the Jim Crow* laws to come about, disenfranchising most blacks *and* many poor whites in the late nineteenth and early twentieth centuries. This challenged the dominant idea that blacks were responsible for their own misfortunes. In this work, Du Bois also demonstrated how black resistance defied the Jim Crow laws and advanced overall humanity in the United States.

In 1950, Du Bois ran for the US Senate to represent New York, campaigning on the position that capitalism* was responsible for racism across the globe. Although Du Bois recognized that the

Soviet Union* had many faults, he defended its political structure of socialism as a potential solution. He was not elected. In 1951 the American government put Du Bois on trial for his growing radicalism and prevented him from travelling abroad until 1958. In an act of defiance he joined the American Communist Party in 1961 and two years later moved to Ghana, a former British colony that had just gained independence. He became a Ghanaian citizen and continued his struggle against global racism from West Africa.

> *"Du Bois ... informed the reader that racism and discrimination not only stymied Blacks, but had serious repercussions for Whites whose fear, doubt, distrust, contempt, and hatred of Blacks diminished their own humanity. Thus the legacy of racism left the entire nation deficient of the basic human qualities on which it was supposedly founded."*
> —— Professor Sandra L. Barnes, Vanderbilt University

Integration

As a scholar, journalist and activist, Du Bois made a lifelong commitment to challenge racism and inequality and to advance the position of blacks in American society. His first seminal work, *The Philadelphia Negro*, written in 1899, provided him with deep insight into the challenges that blacks faced in their pursuit of equality. As he put it,"Merely being born into a group does not necessarily make one possessed of complete knowledge concerning it."[2] He lived among disenfranchised blacks in the American south and became a researcher and teacher on many different aspects of

African American life.

Although he was not yet well acquainted with Marxism* when he wrote *Souls* in 1903, Du Bois nonetheless analyzes the political economy of racism and discusses it as a by-product of capitalism. He also addresses the effects racism has had on the formation of both black and white identities. Du Bois diagnoses "the color line" as the great divider of the twentieth century and introduces his seminal concepts of "double consciousness" and "the veil." Furthermore, he stresses the importance of education and leadership in attaining equal citizenship.

By the time of *Black Reconstruction*, which he wrote 32 years later in 1935, Du Bois had acquired a thorough knowledge of Marxism and he explores the relationship between the industrial economy and racism in some depth. Against the backdrop of the Great Depression*—the worldwide economic depression that lasted from 1929–39—he describes in detail how industrial capitalism creates a system that favors white property-owners over workers, and how racism is a tool the privileged classes use to expand their wealth. He also challenges the dominant idea that the proper emancipation of black people failed during the period of Reconstruction* because blacks were unsuccessful in politics and other areas of society. He argues that, contrary to popular belief, the north was not "the magnanimous emancipator" following the Civil War* and the south was not "a martyr to inescapable fate."[3] Du Bois identifies slavery as the primary cause of the Civil War and the Jim Crow laws that followed as a system that whites knowingly imposed on blacks to safeguard their own interests.

It is evident that Du Bois became more radical over time in response to key world events such as the Russian Revolution,* and the Cold War,* as well as his own experience of racism and inequality. But his entire body of work is united by his struggle for greater democracy and humanity.

Significance

During the course of Du Bois's life he made immense contributions to academia and society. He wrote 21 books, edited 15 more and published over 100 essays and articles.[4] He was also a leader of black civil-rights group the Niagara Movement,* the NAACP, and pan-Africanism, an ideology that encouraged the solidarity of Africans worldwide. *The Souls of Black Folk* was just one important contribution in his lifelong struggle for equality.

Although Du Bois's scholarship is usually associated with sociology it is, in fact, interdisciplinary, covering more than one academic subject. At an American Academy of Political and Social Sciences meeting in 1897 he argued that it was necessary to study "African American problems" in different dimensions by combining historical research, data analysis, anthropological measurement—data taken directly from people about the way they live—and sociological interpretation. Having done exactly that, Du Bois's scholarship has influenced sociology, history, economics, politics, religious studies, art and literature.

At present Du Bois's scholarship lies at the intersection of African American studies, race and ethnicity studies and post-colonial studies. Important scholars like Paul Gilroy* and Homi K.

Bhabha* have revived his ideas about racism and black identity and have applied them to a much broader global context in response to anti-colonial struggles, decolonization (or the undoing of colonialism) and post-colonial immigration. The author's ideas are still important in academia, as well as continuing to inspire social movements globally.

---

1. David Levering Lewis, *W. E. B. Du Bois: Biography of a Race, 1868–1919* (New York: Henry Holt, 1993), 191.

2. W. E. B. Du Bois, *The Autobiography of W. E. B. Du Bois*, (New York: International Publishers, 1968),198.

3. W. E. B. Du Bois, *Black Reconstruction in America* (New York: Russell and Russell, 1963), 723.

4. NAACP History: W. E. B. Du Bois, accessed January 28, 2015, http://www.naacp.org/pages/naacp-history-W. E. B.-dubois.

SECTION 3
IMPACT

THE FIRST RESPONSES

KEY POINTS

* Some anonymous reviewers praised *The Souls of Black Folk* for its great literary and social value. Others expressed mixed feelings. Still more claimed it was a dangerous book because it would ignite further racial tension.

* In 1904, a year after its publication, W. E. B. Du Bois acknowledged that *Souls* had some minor flaws. But he stood by all of the views he had expressed in the book.

* The most important factor that shaped the way people felt about the text was the period when it was written: namely the time of the Jim Crow* laws.*

Criticism

W. E. B. Du Bois's *The Souls of Black Folk* posed a bold challenge to the dominant idea that blacks were biologically and culturally inferior to whites and were responsible for their own failed emancipation during Reconstruction.* Like other Du Bois works, it used powerful and persuasive arguments to show how far from the truth this was.

The immediate response after publication was mixed. On the one hand, some praised *Souls* for its literary and social brilliance, such as one anonymous reviewer from *The Nation* magazine who expressed his awe over the emotional power of the text and its ability to captivate the reader. Another from the *Methodist Magazine and Review* commented on Du Bois's "fine literary grace," while a reviewer from *The Westminster Review* argued that "the work offers a rational solution to the colour problem that has so long perplexed the United States."[1]

On the other hand, some viewed the book as threatening, claiming it would ignite further racial tension. One anonymous reviewer in the *Nashville American* wrote, "This book is indeed dangerous for the Negro to read, for it will only excite discontent and race hatred and fill his imagination with things that do not exist, or things that should not bear upon his mind."Another anonymous reviewer from the *New York Times* criticized Du Bois for attacking Booker T. Washington* and argued that, as a northern black, Du Bois should not be speaking for the American south.[2]

Other critics were ambivalent. An anonymous reviewer from the *American Monthly Review of Reviews* wrote, "No book of similar character has been printed in recent years that equals this little volume in power or grace of expression," but then argued that "as a practical solution for the educational problem of the black race, his essays cannot be regarded as of equal value with the widely published lectures and addresses of Mr. Washington."[3]

> "If Du Bois sincerely feared, as he suggested in 'The After-Thought,' that his book might fall 'still-born into the world wilderness,' reassurance came quickly."
>
> —— Professor David Levering Lewis, New York University

Responses

In 1904 Du Bois published a review of his own work in *The Independent* journal. Although he did not respond directly to criticisms, he did reflect on *Souls* in retrospect. He apologized for the abruptness of certain sections of the text, explaining that since he had written it over the course of seven years he had mixed different styles, tones and ideas. Nevertheless, in conclusion Du Bois stood by his arguments and made it clear that what connected all 14 essays was the idea that America *was* a deeply racist nation and that this racism must be overcome.[4]

The debate between Du Bois and Washington over the direction blacks should take against racism and inequality persisted until Washington's death in 1915. Du Bois continued to argue that only education, leadership, resistance and struggle would bring about equality in American society. In particular, he stressed the need for highly educated blacks like himself to guide the masses in transforming society. While Du Bois's view became more radical over time, the essence of his work was consistent from beginning to end.

Conflict and Consensus

The historical period in which Du Bois published *Souls* shaped its reception. Although some radicals praised Du Bois for his literary and social brilliance, many white southerners criticized him for challenging the status quo, an existing state of affairs that privileged whites and allowed them to expand their wealth.[5]

White southerners saw black political speaker Booker T. Washington as an ally because he was prepared to accommodate the idea that whites were naturally superior and that blacks should submit to them. As a presidential advisor, Washington had some financial control over black education and enjoyed a good reputation among powerful whites, who thought of him as someone who would help them make it acceptable to continue exploiting blacks.

Du Bois referred to Washington's way of dealing with racism as the Tuskegee Machine. Tuskegee in Alabama was where Washington had built a black college as he tried to improve the lot of African Americans. Du Bois did not agree with Washington's belief that cooperation with whites was the way to defeat racism but he recognized that it was very difficult to bring down Washington's stronghold. As Du Bois put it: "Most of the papers found it to their advantage certainly not to oppose Mr. Washington, even if they did not wholly agree with him. Negroes who sought high positions groveled for his favor."[6]

Nevertheless, through his writings, teaching and activism, Du Bois did challenge Washington's position as the leading black intellectual of the time. With his persuasive and scientifically based arguments he managed to make some whites reflect on the situation in America and provide inspiration and impetus for the advancement of blacks in America and elsewhere.

---

1. W. E. B. Du Bois, *The Souls of Black Folk* (New York and London: W.W. Norton and Company, 1999), xx, 221–234.
2. Du Bois, *The Souls of Black Folk*, 26.
3. Albert Shaw, "The New Books: Notes on Recent American Publications," *American Monthly Review of Reviews* 28 (1903): 249.
4. W. E. B. Du Bois, "The Souls of Black Folk," *The Independent* 57 (1904): 2920.
5. Du Bois, *The Souls of Black Folk*, 221–234.
6. W. E. B. Du Bois, *Dusk of Dawn: Essay Towards an Autobiography of a Race* (New York: Harcourt Brace, 1940), 76.

MODULE 10
THE EVOLVING DEBATE

KEY POINTS

* *The Souls of Black Folk* and W. E. B. Du Bois's wider body of work give a detailed analysis of racism in the America of the Jim Crow* laws, encouraging the struggle for equality. This has had a major impact, both in the United States and elsewhere.
* Today Du Bois's legacy lies at the crossroads of black political thought, race and ethnicity studies and post-colonial studies.
* His scholarship has shaped the ideas of prominent scholars such as Paul Gilroy* and Homi K. Bhabha.* Both have extended his concept of "double consciousness" by applying it to post-colonial research.

Uses and Problems

The three key concepts of W. E. B. Du Bois's *The Souls of Black Folk* are "the color line,""double consciousness," and "the veil."

During the course of his life Du Bois's view of "the color line" changed. Whereas in 1903 he portrays it quite narrowly as a marker of division between whites and blacks, in *"The Negro and the Warsaw Ghetto"*[1] in 1952 he explains that he did not fully understand the condition of blacks in the United States until he witnessed how Jews lived in the Warsaw Ghetto* during World War II.* As Du Bois puts it:

"The problem of slavery, emancipation and caste in the United States was no longer in my mind a separate and unique thing as I had long conceived it. It was not even solely a matter of color and physical and racial characteristics ... No, the race problem in which I was interested cut across lines of color and physique and belief and status and was a matter of cultural patterns, perverted teaching and human hate and prejudice, which reached all sorts of people and caused endless evil to all men."[2]

This quote is important because it shows how Du Bois came to understand that racism was more than just a "veil" separating whites and blacks in America. Instead, it shows his understanding of racism as an ever-changing phenomenon that adapts across time. Since then, a wide variety of scholars ranging from Hannah Arendt* to Paul Gilroy have studied the nature of racism and its relationship to other forms of discrimination, such as anti-Semitism* and gender discrimination.

Du Bois first used the term "double consciousness" in 1897's *"Strivings of the Negro People."* He then developed it further in *Souls*. It refers to the identity conflict in being both African and American in a profoundly racist society. As Du Bois observes, "[The African American] simply wishes to make it possible for a man to be both a Negro and an American without being cursed and spit upon by his fellows, without having the doors of opportunity closed roughly in his face."[3]

Du Bois uses the term "the veil" as a metaphor to describe the division between these two consciousnesses (the African and the American) and two societies (white and black). He believes this "color line" is both a curse and a blessing, a danger that can be overcome through struggle and recognition.

Different scholars have applied Du Bois's metaphor of "the color line" and "the veil" to other contexts. One prominent example is Martinique-born African-French writer and revolutionary Frantz Fanon,*who used these concepts in his seminal 1952 work *Black Skin, White Masks* to describe black identity as it is understood by white colonialists. In one passage Fanon describes a young white boy who sees Fanon, points at him and says,"Look, a Negro!" He then jumps in his mother's arms looking for safety. Experiencing this, Fanon feels a painful denial of his own identity. He says, "My body was given back to me sprawled out, distorted, recolored, clad in mourning in that white winter day."[4]

This passage is similar to Du Bois's first encounter with blackness, when he offers a greeting card to a white girl at Fisk University and she refuses to accept it. Du Bois describes his experience as follows:

"Then it dawned upon me with a certain suddenness that I was different from the others; or like [them perhaps] in heart and life and longing, but shut out from their world by a vast veil."[5]

> *"Although our society is more tolerant than ever before, a new form of racism exists — aversive racism — characterized by egalitarian attitudes, but avoidance and subtle discrimination against Blacks. And Blacks continue to face the dilemma of double consciousness. As posited by Cornel West (1993), research confirms that 'race' still matters in terms of opportunity, access, treatment, and quality of life."*
>
> —— Professor Sandra L. Barnes, Vanderbilt University

Schools of Thought

In 1903, Du Bois belonged to two schools of thought. First, he made a major contribution to the development of sociology as an evidence-based discipline. He did this by explaining the material causes of racism against the backdrop of the Jim Crow* laws and how this led to inequality. Second, by opposing Booker T. Washington* and defending social struggle and equality, Du Bois carried on the tradition of those who had fought against slavery like Frederick Douglass.* Du Bois was an integrationist, which means he believed that, by means of social conflict, white and black society could eventually be united into one multicultural unit where democracy and humanity would flourish. In this sense he was a precursor to Martin Luther King,* but found himself at odds with the separatist view of Marcus Garvey,* who set the stage for the Black Power* movement of the 1960s which advocated black separatism.

Today Du Bois's work sits at the intersection of black political thought, race and ethnicity studies and post-colonial studies. His entire body of work focuses on racism and how the oppressed can transcend "the color line." His late works, such as 1961's *Worlds of Color*, move beyond the borders of the United States by calling for the end of colonial domination and global imperialism, which Du Bois associated closely with capitalism.*

In Current Scholarship

Du Bois has influenced many current scholars, in particular Paul Gilroy and Homi K. Bhabha. In his work *The Black Atlantic*, Gilroy extends Du Bois's description of "double consciousness" to people of African descent everywhere. He focuses on how these people have simultaneously been an integral part of history and yet have been violently excluded from that history. He says that they have made immense scientific, literary, political, social and cultural contributions to society and yet whites have cast them as inferior and not allowed them the freedoms of whites or full citizenship. Black intellectuals today are in a position to question injustice and are invested with what Gilroy calls "a special clarity of vision" or "a dreadful objectivity." These black intellectual voices have struggled against racism in the United States and against European colonialism and have successfully questioned the dominant argument of "rational, western progress"—the idea that white western culture is naturally superior.[6]

In *The Location of Culture*, Homi K. Bhabha also builds on Du Bois's concept of "double consciousness" by arguing that a Third Space has emerged where individuals have evolving identities made up of more than one background or culture. This moves beyond the two-part vision put forward by Du Bois, where you are black or white and nothing in between. Bhabha argues that a disruption of these strict barriers means there is an ongoing interchange between the "colonizer" and the "colonized" that can ultimately lead to progress and greater humanity.

1. W. E. B. Du Bois, "The Negro and the Warsaw Ghetto," *Jewish Life* (May 1952).
2. W. E. B. Du Bois, "Social Theory of W. E. B. Du Bois, The Negro and the Warsaw Ghetto," in Phil Zuckerman, *Jewish Life* (Thousand Oaks: Pine Forge Press, 2004), 45–46.
3. W. E. B. Du Bois, *The Souls of Black Folk* (New York and London: W.W. Norton and Company, 1999), 10–11.
4. Frantz Fanon, *Black Skins, White Masks* (London: MacGibbon and Kee, 1968), 113.
5. Du Bois, *The Souls of Black Folk*, 10.
6. Paul Gilroy, *The Black Atlantic: Modernity and Double Consciousness* (London: Verso, 1993), 29, 38–9, 171.

MODULE 11
IMPACT AND INFLUENCE TODAY

KEY POINTS

* *Souls* remains a seminal text within a variety of academic disciplines.
* The text continues to challenge racism and inequalities and to encourage struggle against them.
* Broadly speaking, the book now challenges anyone who is racist or holds a non-critical stance on racism.

Position

In 1999 and 2003 there were commemorations of the 100-year anniversaries of W. E. B. Du Bois's *The Philadelphia Negro*[1] and *The Souls of Black Folk*[2] respectively. In 2005 there were centennial celebrations of black civil rights organization the Niagara Movement,*[3] which Du Bois founded in 1905. Additionally, in 2009 President Barack Obama delivered an address at the 100-year commemoration of the National Association for the Advancement of Colored People (NAACP),[4] which Du Bois co-founded. These milestone celebrations were accompanied by a number of academic journal and book publications,[5] as well as media coverage from newspapers and magazines such as the *New York Times*.[6] All this highlighted the extent to which Du Bois is still very much part of, and indeed an inspiration for, discussions on race, racism, identity, democracy, equality and human rights.

In 2003, the National Black Arts Festival in Atlanta commemorated music, drama and other arts inspired by Du Bois.[7]

In the same year at City University of NewYork's Graduate Center, renowned playwright Thulani Davis* led dramatic readings of different passages of *The Souls of Black Folk* featuring prominent figures, like the actor Danny Glover.[8] There is clearly very strong current interest in reviving and revisiting Du Bois's work.

> *"The 'duality' of African Americans—their double-consciousness— became a signal contribution to the notion of the fragmentation of the self, a defining condition of modernism. The once audacious idea that all identities are multiple is now a commonplace ... Delving into the particular to speak to the universal is what, of course, a classic does. Through his curiously powerful text, the particularity of the Negro became a metaphor, a universal aspect of the human condition. And because of this,* The Souls of Black Folk *continues to speak so compellingly to a new generation of readers today."*
>
> —— Professor Henry Louis Gates Jr., Harvard University

Interaction

When *Souls* was first published in 1903 Du Bois posed a challenge to white supremacy and to Booker T. Washington* and his supporters' accommodationist stance. Broadly speaking, the book today challenges anyone who is racist or holds a non-critical stance on racism. Du Bois believed that racism was a social construction put in place by whites for their own material gain. Examples of non-critical stances include: claims that "multiculturalism" is responsible for social breakdown; the failure to account for the root causes of riots; claims that ethnic minorities are to blame for the discrimination they face; and assertions that Western societies have advanced to a point that they are "post-racial" and ideas of differences between the way races are treated are no longer relevant.

The book is still an important reference point for academics, journalists, and activists who want to understand and explain a number of issues:

- The causes of racism
- How racism shapes identity
- Inequality
- The importance of minority education and leadership
- The role of religion and spirituality in fostering collective resistance
- The legacies of minority struggles globally

The Continuing Debate

Today, Du Bois is still a major influence for scholars of race and ethnicity studies and for post-colonial research. "The color line," "double consciousness," and "the veil" remain important themes in these fields. Psychology professors John F. Dovidio* and Samuel L. Gaertner,* for example, have addressed how discussions about racism have changed since Du Bois published *Souls*. They point to the way racism has become more subtle in the West and is frequently camouflaged by talk of multiculturalism, anti-racism, and egalitarianism.[9]

American sociologist E. Franklin Frazier,* who is also an author on racism, has shown how the equivalent of the rural cabins described by Du Bois as "dirty and dilapidated, smelling of eating and sleeping, poorly ventilated, and anything but homes"[10] are today urban slums characterized by segregation, squalor, and lack of opportunity.[11]

Other scholars such as Douglas Massey* and Nancy Denton* have shown that color-based racism persists to this day, particularly when it comes to the amount of discrimination faced by blacks in the fields of education and employment in modern-day United States. They have argued for economic reform to address a growing sense of angst among lower-class African Americans.[12] American philosopher and public intellectual Cornel West* has asked: why are there so few prominent black leaders such as Du Bois today?[13]

Scholars such as African-American studies expert Andrew Billingsley*[14] and the activist Eric Lincoln*[15] have pointed to the importance of religion in *Souls* and the book's emphasis on striving for greater spiritual humanity. Both feel this is an area of the work that has been overlooked. They highlight the historical role of the black Church as a provider of education, economic aid, and sanctuary and solidarity against racism, gangs, drugs, and poverty. They also highlight the important role of the black church in helping to create black leaders such as Martin Luther King.* All of this shows how the central themes of *Souls* remain relevant in modern scholarship.

---

1. See, for example: Lynn Burbridge, "W. E. B. Du Bois as Economic Analyst: Reflections on the 100th Year Anniversary of The Philadelphia Negro," *Review of Black Political Economy* 26, no. 3 (1999): 13–31.

2. There are too many examples to cite here. Commemoration events took place across the United States.

3. See, for example, Patricia Donovan, "Event to Mark Centennial of Niagara Movement," *University of Buffalo Reporter*, July 7, 2005, accessed January 29, 2015, http://www.buffalo.edu/ubreporter/archive/vol36/vol36n41/articles/NiagaraMovement.html?print=1.

4. "Remarks by the President to the NAACP Centennial Convention," The White House, Office of the Press Secretary, July 17, 2009, accessed January 28, 2015, http://www.whitehouse.gov/the-press-office/remarks-president-naacp-centennial-convention-07162009.

5. See, for example: Dolan Hubbard, *The Souls of Black Folk: 100 Years Later* (Columbia: University of Missouri Press, 2007).

6. Henry Louis Gates Jr., "The Souls of Black Folk at 100: Both Sides Now," *New York Times*, May 4, 2003, accessed January 28, 2015, http://www. nytimes.com/2003/05/04/books/review/04GATEST. html.

7. TaRessa Stovall, "Arts Festival Celebrates W. E. B. Du Bois and the Diaspora," *The Crisis* 110, no. 5 (2003): 48.

8. Press Release: "'Souls of Black Folk: A Centennial Celebration' To Premiere at Graduate Center Stars Featured in Dramatic Readings of Du Bois's Classic Work," January 1, 2003, accessed January 28, 2015, http://www. gc.cuny.edu/News/GC-News/Detail?id=5920.

9. John F. Dovidio and Samuel L. Gaertner, "The Aversive Forms of Racism," in *Prejudice, Discrimination, and Racism,* eds. John F. Dovidio and Samuel L. Gaertner (Orlando: Academic Press, 1986), 61–89.

10. Du Bois, *The Souls of Black Folk*, 91.

11. E. Franklin Frazier, *The Negro Church in America* (Liverpool: Liverpool University Press, 1964).

12. Douglas Massey and Nancy Denton, *American Apartheid: Segregation and the Making of the Underclass* (Massachusetts: Harvard University Press, 1993).

13. Cornel West, "The Dilemma of the Black Intellectual," *Critical Quarterly* 29, no.4 (1987): 39–52.

14. Andrew Billingsley, *Mighty Like a River: The Black Church and Social Reform* (New York: Oxford University Press, 1999).

15. Eric Lincoln, *Race, Religion and the Continuing American Dilemma* (New York: Hill and Wang, 1984).

MODULE 12
WHERE NEXT?

KEY POINTS

* *The Souls of Black Folk* will most likely continue to influence black studies, race and ethnicity studies, and post-colonial studies. It appears W. E. B. Du Bois will remain an important inspiration for social movements globally.

* Du Bois's core concepts—"the color line," "double consciousness," and "the veil"—will probably continue to serve as important reference points for further research.

* The text is seminal because it improves our understanding of racism, how it affects identity, and how we can collectively struggle to overcome it.

Potential

There were large-scale 100-year commemorations of *The Souls of Black Folk* in 2003 and there are strong links in modern scholarship between W. E. B. Du Bois's work and race and ethnicity studies, as well as post-colonial studies. This suggests that this text in particular and Du Bois's wider body of work will continue to be important in the future. His insights on racism in America, its origins in the world of making money, its impact on identity, and the author's hope that America will one day transform "the color line" in order to become truly democratic and achieve greater humanity are timeless, despite being rooted in a particular context of United States history, specifically the Jim Crow* laws. These core issues not only remain relevant in the United States today, but they also apply more broadly. In the future, scholars are likely to continue linking Du Bois to the historical discrimination and inequalities faced by blacks and other minorities, and their struggles to overcome them.

Although *Souls* refers specifically to an American context, Du Bois's later work, ending with the novel *Dark Princess* in 1928, addresses his pan-African* vision of equality. As he puts it, "Africa is, of course, my fatherland ... one thing is sure and that is the fact that since the fifteenth century these ancestors of mine have had a common history, have suffered a common disaster, and have one long memory ... the badge of color is relatively unimportant save as a badge; the real essence of its kinship is the heritage of slavery; the discrimination and insult ... it is this unity that draws me to Africa."[1]

> *"Du Bois understood how change would come—just as [Martin Luther] King* and all the civil rights giants did later. They understood that unjust laws needed to be overturned; that legislation needed to be passed; and that Presidents needed to be pressured into action. They knew that the stain of slavery and the sin of segregation had to be lifted in the courtroom and in the legislature. But they also knew that here, in America, change would have to come from the people ... Because of what they did, we are a more perfect union."*
>
> —— Barack Obama, President of the United States

Future Directions

Although social movements have made much progress over

time,"the color line" remains a major problem in the twenty-first century, even if its nature changes along with political, economic, social, and cultural transformations. Today, racism in America is characterized by the connections between such elements as class, skin color, religion, and gender. As Du Bois made clear when he saw the conditions of Jews in the Warsaw ghetto* during World War II,* racism is a much broader and more complex phenomenon than the one he depicted in his earlier works. Through his own personal journey from Great Barrington, Massachusetts, to Ghana his outlook matured and he came to understand the various dimensions of racism much better. In the future, this theme and its links with the formation of identity, human rights, resistance, struggle, and negotiation will likely continue to be explored by students, scholars, journalists, and activists. Those who study race and ethnicity, and post-colonialism such as Paul Gilroy* and Homi K. Bhabha,* are examples. However, the text is interdisciplinary, affecting different academic fields of study, and could benefit from greater attention from other fields such as religious studies.

Summary

The Souls of Black Folk is an essential read for anyone who wants to understand American and African-American history better. Du Bois built on the legacy of the former slave Frederick Douglass* by providing a detailed, scientifically based analysis of slavery, the American Civil War,* the Emancipation Proclamation,* the Reconstruction* era, and Jim Crow* discrimination. Despite having the right to vote and having been awarded other important freedoms in the Thirteenth, Fourteenth, and Fifteenth Amendments to the Constitution,* these Jim Crow laws ultimately re-enslaved blacks.

The text also provides significant insight into the social construction of race as a means to advance white economic interests and challenges the dominant argument of the times that blacks were biologically and culturally inferior to whites. It also details the effects of racism on black identity.

Throughout *Souls*, Du Bois aims to be the new leader of "the Negro cause" by urging blacks to be proud of their culture and to draw from their spirituality. He drives black people to engage collectively in social struggle so that whites will acknowledge their past injustices and recognize blacks as equals. Du Bois hopes that by this means African Americans will eventually be able to lift "the veil," overcome the tormenting condition of "double consciousness," and help whites make America the great democracy it claims to be— that is,"one nation, indivisible, under God."

It is likely that the book's three most important concepts—"the color line," "double consciousness," and "the veil"—will remain fundamental for a long time to come, not just in sociology, but in many fields ranging from anthropology to history to economics to politics. The book will probably also remain at the heart of race and ethnicity studies and postcolonial analyses, the main reason being that racism—against a backdrop of capitalism—continues to exist and affect identity. It can only be overcome—as Du Bois so persuasively argued in 1903—through education, leadership, and social conflict. The issues may have changed, subtly or otherwise, but the "color line" continues to be very much a problem of the twenty-first century.

---

1. W. E. B. Du Bois, *Dusk of Dawn: Essay Towards an Autobiography of a Race* (New York: Harcourt Brace, 1940), 116.

GLOSSARY OF TERMS

1. **Abolition:** refers to the end of slavery in the United States.

2. **Abolitionist Movement:** refers to the movement before the American Civil War to end slavery.

3. **American Civil War:** a war fought in the United States between northern (Union) and southern (Confederate) states from 1861 to 1865.

4. **Anti-Semitism:** prejudice or hostility towards Jews.

5. **Atlanta Compromise:** an agreement made in Atlanta in 1895 that established that blacks would submit to white racism and political rule in exchange for basic legal rights and a basic education.

6. **Atlantic Monthly:** founded in Boston in 1857, this is one of the oldest and most respected magazines in the United States.

7. **Black is Beautiful:** a cultural movement that began in the United States in the 1960s which sought to dispel the myth that black physical features were less beautiful than white ones.

8. **Black Codes:** laws passed in former confederate states to restrict the activity of freed black and ensure their availability as a labour force following the abolition of slavery.

9. **Black Nationalism:** the idea that blacks should separate from white society and govern themselves.

10. **Black Power:** a political movement that began in the United States in the 1960s that encouraged black separatism.

11. **Capitalism:** an economic system that emphasizes the private ownership of the means of production. Du Bois argued that there was a strong link between capitalism and racism.

12. **Civilizing Mission:** the doctrine upon which European colonialism operated, justifying exploitation in the colonies by claiming Europe had been given the duty to civilize "the uncivilized."

13. **Cold War:** the state of political hostility that existed between the Warsaw Pact (Soviet Union and its allies) and North Atlantic Treaty Organization from 1945

to 1990.

14. **Communism:** a political ideology that relies on the state ownership of the means of production, the collectivization of labor, and the abolition of social class.

15. **Congress:** the national legislative body of the United States, comprised of the Senate and the House of Representatives. Congress passed the Fifteenth Amendment in 1870, granting African Americans the right to vote.

16. **Consciousness:** according to Hegel, consciousness is the awareness of another's awareness of oneself. In other words, we see ourselves through the eyes of others.

17. **Constitution:** a set of principles upon which a state is recognized to be founded. The US Constitution, signed in 1787, replaced the Articles of Confederation with a stronger central government.

18. **Declaration of the Rights of Man and of the Citizen:** a document signed by the French National Constituent Assembly in 1789. It stresses that all men are naturally equal, and thus have equal rights under the law.

19. **Elegy:** a poem of mourning and reverence.

20. **Emancipation Proclamation:** a political proclamation made by President Abraham Lincoln in 1863 in the middle of the Civil War. It established that all persons held as slaves in the rebellious southern states would be free from that moment on.

21. **Enlightenment:** a cultural and intellectual movement in the seventeenth and eighteenth centuries that looked to reform society through the use of reason. This provided the "scientific" backdrop for the work of Herbert Spencer and Charles Darwin, who argued that blacks were biologically and culturally inferior to whites.

22. **Evolutionary Biology:** a field of academic inquiry concerned with the evolutionary processes that produce the diversity of life on Earth. When W. E. B. Du Bois published *Souls*, the dominant view in the social sciences was that blacks were biologically inferior to whites.

23. **Freedman's Bureau:** a federal agency from 1865 to 1872 that integrated freed slaves by providing them with educational services, legal counsel, and

employment aid.

24. **French Revolution:** a period of political and social upheaval in France that began in 1789 with the popular overthrow of the monarchy and ended in 1799 with the rise of Napoleon.

25. **Great Depression:** the global financial crisis that began in 1929 and continued until World War II.

26. **Great Man Theory:** a theory which argues that great men use their intelligence, wisdom, charisma, and political acumen to transform history.

27. **Jim Crow Laws:** a period in American history from the end of Reconstruction in1877 until the civil rights movements of the 1950s and 1960s. State and federal governments put a number of laws in place to stop blacks from attaining greater equality. Du Bois published *The Souls of Black Folk* during this era.

28. **Ku Klux Klan:** a secret society founded in the United States in 1866 that reasserted white supremacy through violence.

29. **Literacy Test:** a test used during the period of Jim Crow by some states and local governments as part of the voting registration process for blacks. Those who could not read or could not pass the test were denied their right to vote, as allowed in the Fifteenth Amendment.

30. **Marxism:** the name given to the political system advocated by Karl Marx. It emphasised an end to capitalism by taking control of the means of production from individuals and placing it in the hands of central government.

31. **National Association for the Advancement of Colored People (NAACP):** a black civil rights organization formed by W. E. B. Du Bois, Moorfield Storey and Mary White Ovington in 1909. It worked to end racism and achieve equality.

32. **Naturalist:** a person who studies or is an expert in natural history, for example Charles Darwin. His views were very influential when W. E. B. Du Bois published *Souls*.

33. **Niagara Movement:** a black civil rights organization founded by W. E. B. Du Bois and William Monroe Trotter in 1905. It opposed the accommodationist stance of Booker T. Washington, and called for an end to racial segregation.

34. ***On the Origin of Species***: a seminal work published in 1859 by naturalist Charles Darwin. It is widely considered to be the foundation of evolutionary biology, which shaped the dominant view when W. E. B. Du Bois published *Souls* that blacks were biologically inferior to whites.

35. **Pan-Africanism:** the idea that all people of African descent have common interests and should unite.

36. ***Plessy versus Ferguson***: a landmark court case in the United States in 1896 that upheld the right of state and local governments to practice segregation under the doctrine of "separate but equal."

37. **Poll Taxes:** a tax levied as a prerequisite for voting. During the period of Jim Crow some states and local governments implemented a tax, which prevented blacks who couldn't or didn't want to pay it from exercising their right to vote, as stipulated in the Fifteenth Amendment.

38. **Protestant:** a Christian whose faith and practice are founded on the principles of the Reformation. W. E. B. Du Bois had a Protestant upbringing.

39. **Reconstruction:** the period from 1865 to 1877 when the federal government of the United States reincorporated the southern states into the Union.

40. **Russian Revolution:** a series of revolutions in Russia in 1917 that destroyed the Tsar's ruling authority and led to the creation of the Soviet Union. Du Bois studied the Russian Revolution and travelled to Russia in 1927.

41. **Scientific Method:** a method of investigation whereby a problem is first identified and observations and experiments are then carried out to construct ways to solve it. W. E. B. Du Bois applied the scientific method to his seminal works.

42. **Soviet Union:** a federal socialist republic officially known as the Union of Soviet Socialist Republics that existed between 1922 and 1991.

43. **Talented Tenth:** a term used by Du Bois to refer to a well-educated elite group of black leaders who could lead the masses in their struggle for equality. It is based on the assumption that one in 10 black people could become such leaders.

44. **Universal Negro Improvement Association:** a fraternal association founded

in 1914 that aimed to encourage solidarity among blacks so that they could separate from white society and govern themselves.

45. **Valley of the Shadow of Death:** a phrase used in Psalm 23:4 of the Bible. It refers to a situation of grave danger, in which hope still exists if one fears no evil. Du Bois believed that although blacks suffer great discrimination, their resistance and struggle would eventually lead them to overcome prejudice.

46. **Warsaw Ghetto:** the largest of the Jewish ghettoes in occupied Europe during World War II.

47. **World War II (1939–45):** global war between the vast majority of world states, including all the great powers of the time.

1. **Hannah Arendt (1906–75)** was one of the most famous political theorists of the twentieth century. She was staunchly anti-totalitarian and supportive of freedom and analyzed the relationship between different forms of discrimination.

2. **Homi K. Bhabha (b. 1949)** is Anne F. Rothenberg Professor of English and American Literature and Language, and the Director of the Humanities Center at Harvard University. In his work *The Location of Culture*, Bhabha extended Du Bois's ideas about double-consciousness to argue that in the postcolonial era there is a Third Space of people who exist between "the colonizer" and "the colonized."

3. **Andrew Billingsley** is a sociologist and renowned scholar of black studies at the University of South Carolina. He has argued that *Souls* provides great insight into black spirituality, which he claims has been largely overlooked in scholarly literature.

4. **Thomas Carlyle (1795–1881)** was a Scottish philosopher and historian. His book *On Heroes, Hero-Worship, and the Heroic in History* argued that great men transform history through their intelligence, wisdom, charisma, and political acumen.

5. **Auguste Comte (1798–1857)** was a French philosopher, the founder of sociology and the doctrine of positivism which argues that knowledge can be scientifically tested.

6. **Charles Darwin (1809–82)** was a British naturalist and geologist considered to be the father of the evolutionary theory, which challenged the idea that God created the universe.

7. **Thulani Davis (b. 1949)** is a well-known American writer and playwright. She has performed dramatic readings of W. E. B. Du Bois's writings in theaters in the United States.

8. **Nancy Denton** is a professor of sociology at the University of Albany, who has published work on segregation in the United States, including *American Apartheid*. She has highlighted the importance of *Souls* with regard to racism

and black identity, and claims that racism is still a major problem in American society.

9. **Frederick Douglass (1818–95)** was an escaped slave who became a writer, orator, statesman, and leader in the abolitionist movement to outlaw slavery in the United States.

10. **John F. Dovidio** is a professor of psychology at Yale University. He argues that the discourse of racism has changed since W. E. B. Du Bois published *Souls*; he claims that racism today is more subtle, and is codified as multiculturalism, anti-racism, and egalitarianism.

11. **Ralph Waldo Emerson (1803–82)** was a well-known American writer and philosopher of the nineteenth century who championed transcendentalism or the idea that philosophy and literature should challenge the current state of society and culture. In his work he coined the term "double consciousness," though he did not relate it to African Americans, as Du Bois did.

12. **Frantz Fanon (1925–61)** was a Martinique-born Afro-French philosopher and revolutionary who wrote *The Wretched of the Earth* and *Black Skin, White Masks*. W. E. B. Du Bois influenced his work on racism and black identity.

13. **E. Franklin Frazier (1894–1962)** was an American sociologist and author who wrote many books on blacks in America, including *The Negro Family in the United States*. He has argued that the segregation, squalor, and lack of opportunity that W. E. B. Du Bois describes in *Souls* in rural areas now occurs in cities.

14. **Samuel L. Gaertner** is a professor of psychology at the University of Delaware. He argues that the discourse of racism has changed since W. E. B. Du Bois published *Souls*; he claims that today it is more subtle, and is codified as multiculturalism, anti-racism, and egalitarianism.

15. **Marcus Garvey (1887–1940)** was a Jamaican political leader who promoted the cause of Black Nationalism, in which whites and blacks would live in separate societies. He was the founder of the Black Star Line, which hoped to return all people of African descent to Africa.

16. **Paul Gilroy (b. 1956)** is a professor of American and English Literature at King's College London. Gilroy's *The Black Atlantic* extends the ideas of Du Bois by linking the lived experiences of racism of black people globally.

17. **Ulysses Grant (1822–85)** was an army general and president of the United States from 1869 to1877. He led the Union army to victory in the Civil War and was president during Reconstruction.

18. **G. W. F. Hegel (1770–1831)** was a German philosopher whose theories heavily influenced Karl Marx. In *Souls*, Du Bois adapted Hegel's link between history and consciousness in *The Phenomenology of the Spirit* to the condition of African Americans in the United States.

19. **Henry James (1843–1916)** was a well-known British-American writer who wrote *The Portrait of a Lady* and *The Turn of the Screw*. He praised W. E. B. Du Bois for his literary brilliance in *Souls*.

20. **Rudyard Kipling (1865–1936)** was an Indian-born English writer, one of the most popular in the nineteenth and twentieth centuries. He is the author of the poem "The White Man's Burden," in which he argues that colonialism is a noble mission because the white man has been given the responsibility of civilizing the black man.

21. **Martin Luther King Jr. (1929–68)** was a Baptist minister and activist who led the civil rights movements in the United States from the 1950s until his assassination in 1968. King built on the legacy of Du Bois, who had co-founded the Niagara Movement and the NAACP.

22. **David Levering Lewis (b. 1936)** is a professor of history at New York University who has won two Pulitzer prizes for his two-part biography of W. E. B. Du Bois.

23. **Abraham Lincoln (1809–65)** was president of the United States from 1861 until his assassination in 1865. He led the country through the Civil War and abolished slavery.

24. **Eric Lincoln (1924–2000)** was an African-American scholar who taught at

several institutions in the United States, including Duke University. He argues that *Souls* provides great insight into black spirituality, which he claims has been largely overlooked in scholarly literature.

25. **Karl Marx (1818–83)** was a German philosopher, economist, historian and sociologist, widely considered one of history's most influential social scientists. Although Du Bois only had a basic understanding of Marxism when he wrote *Souls*, his later works such as *Black Reconstruction* reflect a much deeper understanding of the relationship between capitalism and racism.

26. **Douglas Massey (b. 1952)** is a professor of sociology at Princeton University. He has highlighted the importance of W. E. B. Du Bois's work, and has made clear in his own work that racism is still a major problem in American society.

27. **Herbert Spencer (1820–1903)** was an English philosopher, biologist and sociologist who was an important figure in the domain of evolutionary theory before Charles Darwin. He coined the term "the survival of the fittest."

28. **Booker T. Washington (1856–1915)** was the most prominent black leader in America from 1890 to 1915. He argued that blacks should accept white racism and political rule in exchange for basic legal rights and a basic education, a position that W. E. B. Du Bois firmly opposed.

29. **Max Weber (1864–1920)** was a German philosopher, sociologist, and political economist who deeply influenced social theory, social research, and sociology. When Du Bois studied in Berlin he came into contact with Weber and studied his ideas.

30. **Cornel West (b. 1953)** was the first black PhD graduate in philosophy from Princeton University, and is a prominent intellectual in the United States today. He has highlighted the importance of W. E. B. Du Bois's work, and has asked: why are there so few black figures like Du Bois today?

31. **Robert Wortham** is a professor of sociology at North Carolina Central University. He argued that sociologists often overlook the great contributions of W. E. B. Du Bois.

32. **Earl Wright** is a professor of African studies at the University of Cincinnati. He is an expert on the scholarship of W. E. B. Du Bois.

33. **Shamoon Zamir** is a professor of literature and visual studies at New York University, Abu Dhabi. He has written a book entitled *Dark Voices:W. E. B. Du Bois and American Thought: 1888–1903*.

 **WORKS CITED**

1. Aptheker, Herbert, ed. *The Correspondence of W. E. B. Du Bois: Volume III, Selections 1944–1963*. Amherst: University of Massachusetts Press, 1978.

2. Barnes, Sandra L. "A Sociological Examination of W. E. B. Du Bois' The Souls of Black Folk." *The North Star, A Journal of African American Religious History* 6 (2003): 2.

3. Billingsley, Andrew. *Mighty Like a River: The Black Church and Social Reform*. New York: Oxford University Press, 1999.

4. Burbridge, Lynn. "W. E. B. Du Bois as Economic Analyst: Reflections on the 100th Year Anniversary of The Philadelphia Negro." *The Review of Black Political Economy* 26, no. 3 (1999): 13–31.

5. Comte, Auguste. *Comte: Early Political Writings*. Edited by H. S. Jones. Cambridge: Cambridge University Press, 1998.

6. Darwin, Charles. *The Descent of Man*. London: John Murray, 1871.

7. Donovan, Patricia. "Event to Mark Centennial of Niagara Movement." *University of Buffalo Reporter*, July 7, 2005. Accessed January 29, 2015. http://www.buffalo.edu/ubreporter/archive/vol36/vol36n41/articles/NiagaraMovement.html?print=1.

8. Douglass, Frederick. "The Color Line." *The North American Review* 132 (1881): 567–577.

9. ———. *Narrative of the Life of Frederick Douglass: An American Slave*. Edited by Benjamin Quarles. Cambridge, MA: Harvard University Press, 1988.

10. Dovidio John F. and Samuel L. Gaertner. "The Aversive Forms of Racism." In *Prejudice, Discrimination, and Racism*, edited by John F. Dovidio and Samuel L. Gaertner, 61–89. Orlando: Academic Press, 1986.

11. Du Bois, W. E. B. *An Appeal to the World: A Statement of Denial of Human Rights to Minorities in the Case of Citizens of Negro Descent in the United States of America and an Appeal to the United Nations for Redress*. New York: National Association for the Advancement of Colored People, 1947.

12. ———. *The Autobiography of W. E. B. Du Bois: A Soliloquy on Viewing My Life from the Last Decade of Its First Century*. New York: International Publishers, 1968.

13. ———. *Black Reconstruction in America*. New York: Russell and Russell, 1963.

14. ———. *Darkwater: Voices From Within the Veil*. New York: Harcourt, Brace,

and Howe, 1920.

15. ———. *Dusk of Dawn: Essay Towards an Autobiography of a Race*. New York: Harcourt Brace, 1940.

16. ———. "The Negro and the Warsaw Ghetto." *Jewish Life* 6, no. 7 (1952): 14–15.

17. ———. *The Philadelphia Negro: A Social Study*. New York: Schocken Books, 1967.

18. ———. "Social Theory of W. E. B. Du Bois, The Negro and the Warsaw Ghetto." In Phil Zuckerman, *Jewish Life,* 45–6. Thousand Oaks: Pine Forge Press, 2004.

19. ———. "The Souls of Black Folk." *The Independent* 57 (1904): 2920.

20. ———. *The Souls of Black Folk*. Edited by Henry Louis Gates Jr. and Terri Hume Oliver. New York and London: W. W. Norton and Company, 1999.

21. ———. *The Suppression of the African Slave Trade in the United States of America, 1638–1870*. New York: The Social Science Press, 1954.

22. Fanon, Frantz. *Black Skins, White Masks*. London: MacGibbon and Kee, 1968.

23. Frazier, E. Franklin. *The Negro Church in America*. Liverpool: Liverpool University Press, 1964.

24. Gates Jr., Henry Louis. "The Souls of Black Folk at 100: Both Sides Now." *New York Times*, May 4, 2003. Accessed January 28, 2015. http://www. nytimes. com/2003/05/04/books/review/04GATEST.html.

25. Gilroy, Paul. *The Black Atlantic: Modernity and Double Consciousness*. London: Verso, 1993.

26. Hubbard, Dolan. *The Souls of Black Folk: 100 Years Later*. Columbia: University of Missouri Press, 2007.

27. Johnson, Greg. "W. E. B. Du Bois's The Philadelphia Negro." *Penn Current*, July 2, 2009. Accessed January 20, 2015. http://www.upenn.edu/pennnews/ current/ node/3997.

28. King Jr., Martin Luther. "Honoring Du Bois." The Centennial Address at Carnegie Hall in New York City, February 23, 1968.

29. Kipling, Rudyard. "The White Man's Burden." *McClure's Magazine* 12 (1899): 290–1.

30. Kousser, J. Morgan. *The Shaping of Southern Politics: Suffrage, Restriction and the Establishment of the One-Party South*, 1880–1910. New Haven: Yale University Press, 1974.

31. Lewis, David Levering. *W. E. B. Du Bois: Biography of a Race, 1868–1919*. New York: Henry Holt, 1993.

32. Lincoln, Eric. *Race, Religion and the Continuing American Dilemma*. New York: Hill and Wang, 1984.

33. Massey, Douglas and Nancy Denton. *American Apartheid: Segregation and the Making of the Underclass*. Cambridge, MA: Harvard University Press, 1993.

34. Obama, Barack. "Obama's NAACP Speech." The White House, Office of the Press Secretary. New York, July 16, 2009. Accessed January 28, 2015. http://www.whitehouse.gov/the-press-office/remarks-president-naacp-centennial-convention-07162009.

35. Sayad, Abdelmalek. *The Suffering of the Immigrant*. London: Polity, 2004.

36. Shaw, Albert. "The New Books: Notes on Recent American Publications." *American Monthly Review of Reviews* 28 (1903): 249.

37. Stovall, TaRessa. "Arts Festival Celebrates W. E. B. Du Bois and the Diaspora." *The Crisis* 110, no. 5 (2003): 48.

38. Wamba, Philippe. *Kinship: A Family's Journey in Africa and America*. New York: Dutton, 1999.

39. West, Cornel. "The Dilemma of the Black Intellectual." *Critical Quarterly* 29, no. 4 (1987): 39–52.

40. Wortham, Robert A. "Introduction to the Sociology of W. E. B. Du Bois." *Sociation Today* 3 (2005): 1.

41. Wright, Earl. "W. E. B. Du Bois and the Atlanta Sociological Laboratory." *Sociation Today* 3 (2005): 1.

42. Zamir, Shamoon. *Dark Voices: W. E. B. Du Bois and American Thought: 1888–1903*. Chicago: University of Chicago, 1995.

原书作者简介

　　W. E. B.杜波依斯生于 1868 年，属于马萨诸塞州一个拥有土地的自由黑人小群体。他是一位优秀的学者，也是第一位获得哈佛大学博士学位的非裔美国人。然而，杜波依斯在美国南方学习时亲身经历的种族主义，使他下定决心促进种族平等。无论是作为一名教师、记者，还是政治活动家，他都身体力行并实践终生。杜波依斯在新独立的加纳去世，享年95 岁。

本书作者简介

　　詹森·克西迪亚斯博士在伦敦国王学院获得欧洲政治学博士学位，在那里他完成了关于英国和法国移民和公民身份比较的论文。他曾是加州大学伯克利分校欧洲政治学访问学者。目前，他是纽约大学的政治学讲师。

世界名著中的批判性思维

　　《世界思想宝库钥匙丛书》致力于深入浅出地阐释全世界著名思想家的观点，不论是谁、在何处都能了解到，从而推进批判性思维发展。

　　《世界思想宝库钥匙丛书》与世界顶尖大学的一流学者合作，为一系列学科中最有影响的著作推出新的分析文本，介绍其观点和影响。在这一不断扩展的系列中，每种选入的著作都代表了历经时间考验的思想典范。通过为这些著作提供必要背景、揭示原作者的学术渊源以及说明这些著作所产生的影响，本系列图书希望让读者以新视角看待这些划时代的经典之作。读者应学会思考、运用并挑战这些著作中的观点，而不是简单接受它们。

ABOUT THE AUTHOR OF THE ORIGINAL WORK

W. E. B. Du Bois was born in 1868, part of a small, free, land-owning black population in Massachusetts. He was an excellent scholar and became the first African American to earn a PhD from Harvard University. Yet Du Bois had experienced racism first hand, especially when studying in the American South. That made him determined to promote equality throughout his life as a teacher, journalist, and political activist. Du Bois died at the grand age of 95 in the newly-independent Ghana.

ABOUT THE AUTHOR OF THE ANALYSIS

Dr Jason Xidias holds a PhD in European Politics from King's College London, where he completed a comparative dissertation on immigration and citizenship in Britain and France. He was also a Visiting Fellow in European Politics at the University of California, Berkeley. Currently, he is Lecturer in Political Science at New York University.

ABOUT MACAT
GREAT WORKS FOR CRITICAL THINKING

Macat is focused on making the ideas of the world's great thinkers accessible and comprehensible to everybody, everywhere, in ways that promote the development of enhanced critical thinking skills.

It works with leading academics from the world's top universities to produce new analyses that focus on the ideas and the impact of the most influential works ever written across a wide variety of academic disciplines. Each of the works that sit at the heart of its growing library is an enduring example of great thinking. But by setting them in context — and looking at the influences that shaped their authors, as well as the responses they provoked — Macat encourages readers to look at these classics and game-changers with fresh eyes. Readers learn to think, engage and challenge their ideas, rather than simply accepting them.

批判性思维与《黑人的灵魂》

首要批判性思维技巧：推理

次要批判性思维技巧：创造性思维

W. E. B.杜波依斯的《黑人的灵魂》是社会领域的一部开创性著作和美国文学的经典之作，也是缜密推理的一个坚实例子。

作为美国历史上最重要的关于种族主义与黑人身份的著作之一，该书包含了强有力的论据，阐明了20世纪初美国黑人的地位问题。杜波依斯指出了三个重要的问题（"肤色界线"、"双重意识"和"面纱"），它们才是真正的黑人解放的障碍，并且阐明这些因素如何反过来加剧了不平等问题。

杜波依斯仔细研究了这三个问题，清晰地解释了它们在影响一个遭受系统性歧视群体的意识方面的重要意义，并自始至终出色地处理了反驳意见。《黑人的灵魂》继续深刻地影响了美国的民权运动，激励了世界各地的后殖民思想。

CRITICAL THINKING AND *THE SOULS OF BLACK FOLK*

- Primary critical thinking skill: REASONING
- Secondary critical thinking skill: CREATIVE THINKING

W.E.B Du Bois' *The Souls of Black Folk* is a seminal work in the field of sociology, a classic of American literature—and a solid example of carefully-structured reasoning.

One of the most important texts ever written on racism and black identity in America, the work contains powerful arguments that illustrate the problem of the position of black people in the US at the turn of the 20th-century. Du Bois identified three significant issues ('the color line';'double consciousness'; and 'the veil') that acted as roadblocks to true black emancipation, and showed how each of these in turn contributed to the problem of inequality.

Du Bois carefully investigates all three problems, constructing clear explanations of their significance in shaping the consciousness of a community that has been systematically discriminated against, and dealing brilliantly with counter-arguments throughout. *The Souls of Black Folk* went on to profoundly influence the civil rights movement in the US, inspiring post-colonial thinking worldwide.

《世界思想宝库钥匙丛书》简介

《世界思想宝库钥匙丛书》致力于为一系列在各领域产生重大影响的人文社科类经典著作提供独特的学术探讨。每一本读物都不仅仅是原经典著作的内容摘要，而是介绍并深入研究原经典著作的学术渊源、主要观点和历史影响。这一丛书的目的是提供一套学习资料，以促进读者掌握批判性思维，从而更全面、深刻地去理解重要思想。

每一本读物分为 3 个部分：学术渊源、学术思想和学术影响，每个部分下有 4 个小节。这些章节旨在从各个方面研究原经典著作及其反响。

由于独特的体例，每一本读物不但易于阅读，而且另有一项优点：所有读物的编排体例相同，读者在进行某个知识层面的调查或研究时可交叉参阅多本该丛书中的相关读物，从而开启跨领域研究的路径。

为了方便阅读，每本读物最后还列出了术语表和人名表（在书中则以星号＊标记），此外还有参考文献。

《世界思想宝库钥匙丛书》与剑桥大学合作，理清了批判性思维的要点，即如何通过 6 种技能来进行有效思考。其中 3 种技能让我们能够理解问题，另 3 种技能让我们有能力解决问题。这 6 种技能合称为"批判性思维 PACIER 模式"，它们是：

分析：了解如何建立一个观点；
评估：研究一个观点的优点和缺点；
阐释：对意义所产生的问题加以理解；
创造性思维：提出新的见解，发现新的联系；
解决问题：提出切实有效的解决办法；
理性化思维：创建有说服力的观点。

THE MACAT LIBRARY

The Macat Library is a series of unique academic explorations of seminal works in the humanities and social sciences — books and papers that have had a significant and widely recognised impact on their disciplines. It has been created to serve as much more than just a summary of what lies between the covers of a great book. It illuminates and explores the influences on, ideas of, and impact of that book. Our goal is to offer a learning resource that encourages critical thinking and fosters a better, deeper understanding of important ideas.

Each publication is divided into three Sections: Influences, Ideas, and Impact. Each Section has four Modules. These explore every important facet of the work, and the responses to it.

This Section-Module structure makes a Macat Library book easy to use, but it has another important feature. Because each Macat book is written to the same format, it is possible (and encouraged!) to cross-reference multiple Macat books along the same lines of inquiry or research. This allows the reader to open up interesting interdisciplinary pathways.

To further aid your reading, lists of glossary terms and people mentioned are included at the end of this book (these are indicated by an asterisk [*] throughout) — as well as a list of works cited.

Macat has worked with the University of Cambridge to identify the elements of critical thinking and understand the ways in which six different skills combine to enable effective thinking.

Three allow us to fully understand a problem; three more give us the tools to solve it. Together, these six skills make up the PACIER model of critical thinking. They are:

ANALYSIS — understanding how an argument is built
EVALUATION — exploring the strengths and weaknesses of an argument
INTERPRETATION — understanding issues of meaning
CREATIVE THINKING — coming up with new ideas and fresh connections
PROBLEM-SOLVING — producing strong solutions
REASONING — creating strong arguments

"《世界思想宝库钥匙丛书》提供了独一无二的跨学科学习和研究工具。它介绍那些革新了各自学科研究的经典著作，还邀请全世界一流专家和教育机构进行严谨的分析，为每位读者打开世界顶级教育的大门。"

—— 安德烈亚斯·施莱歇尔，
经济合作与发展组织教育与技能司司长

"《世界思想宝库钥匙丛书》直面大学教育的巨大挑战……他们组建了一支精干而活跃的学者队伍，来推出在研究广度上颇具新意的教学材料。"

—— 布罗尔斯教授、勋爵，剑桥大学前校长

"《世界思想宝库钥匙丛书》的愿景令人赞叹。它通过分析和阐释那些曾深刻影响人类思想以及社会、经济发展的经典文本，提供了新的学习方法。它推动批判性思维，这对于任何社会和经济体来说都是至关重要的。这就是未来的学习方法。"

—— 查尔斯·克拉克阁下，英国前教育大臣

"对于那些影响了各自领域的著作，《世界思想宝库钥匙丛书》能让人们立即了解到围绕那些著作展开的评论性言论，这让该系列图书成为在这些领域从事研究的师生们不可或缺的资源。"

—— 威廉·特朗佐教授，加利福尼亚大学圣地亚哥分校

"Macat offers an amazing first-of-its-kind tool for interdisciplinary learning and research. Its focus on works that transformed their disciplines and its rigorous approach, drawing on the world's leading experts and educational institutions, opens up a world-class education to anyone."

—— Andreas Schleicher, Director for Education and Skills, Organisation for Economic Co-operation and Development

"Macat is taking on some of the major challenges in university education... They have drawn together a strong team of active academics who are producing teaching materials that are novel in the breadth of their approach."

—— Prof Lord Broers, former Vice-Chancellor of the University of Cambridge

"The Macat vision is exceptionally exciting. It focuses upon new modes of learning which analyse and explain seminal texts which have profoundly influenced world thinking and so social and economic development. It promotes the kind of critical thinking which is essential for any society and economy. This is the learning of the future."

—— Rt Hon Charles Clarke, former UK Secretary of State for Education

"The Macat analyses provide immediate access to the critical conversation surrounding the books that have shaped their respective discipline, which will make them an invaluable resource to all of those, students and teachers, working in the field."

—— Prof William Tronzo, University of California at San Diego

The Macat Library
世界思想宝库钥匙丛书

TITLE	中文书名	类别
An Analysis of Arjun Appadurai's *Modernity at Large: Cultural Dimensions of Globalization*	解析阿尔君·阿帕杜莱《消失的现代性：全球化的文化维度》	人类学
An Analysis of Claude Lévi-Strauss's *Structural Anthropology*	解析克劳德·列维—施特劳斯《结构人类学》	人类学
An Analysis of Marcel Mauss's *The Gift*	解析马塞尔·莫斯《礼物》	人类学
An Analysis of Jared M. Diamond's *Guns, Germs, and Steel: The Fate of Human Societies*	解析贾雷德·M.戴蒙德《枪炮、病菌与钢铁：人类社会的命运》	人类学
An Analysis of Clifford Geertz's *The Interpretation of Cultures*	解析克利福德·格尔茨《文化的解释》	人类学
An Analysis of Philippe Ariès's *Centuries of Childhood: A Social History of Family Life*	解析菲力浦·阿利埃斯《儿童的世纪：旧制度下的儿童和家庭生活》	人类学
An Analysis of W. Chan Kim & Renée Mauborgne's *Blue Ocean Strategy*	解析金伟灿/勒妮·莫博涅《蓝海战略》	商业
An Analysis of John P. Kotter's *Leading Change*	解析约翰·P.科特《领导变革》	商业
An Analysis of Michael E. Porter's *Competitive Strategy: Techniques for Analyzing Industries and Competitors*	解析迈克尔·E.波特《竞争战略：分析产业和竞争对手的技术》	商业
An Analysis of Jean Lave & Etienne Wenger's *Situated Learning: Legitimate Peripheral Participation*	解析琼·莱夫/艾蒂纳·温格《情境学习：合法的边缘性参与》	商业
An Analysis of Douglas McGregor's *The Human Side of Enterprise*	解析道格拉斯·麦格雷戈《企业的人性面》	商业
An Analysis of Milton Friedman's *Capitalism and Freedom*	解析米尔顿·弗里德曼《资本主义与自由》	商业
An Analysis of Ludwig von Mises's *The Theory of Money and Credit*	解析路德维希·冯·米塞斯《货币和信用理论》	经济学
An Analysis of Adam Smith's *The Wealth of Nations*	解析亚当·斯密《国富论》	经济学
An Analysis of Thomas Piketty's *Capital in the Twenty-First Century*	解析托马斯·皮凯蒂《21世纪资本论》	经济学
An Analysis of Nassim Nicholas Taleb's *The Black Swan: The Impact of the Highly Improbable*	解析纳西姆·尼古拉斯·塔勒布《黑天鹅：如何应对不可预知的未来》	经济学
An Analysis of Ha-Joon Chang's *Kicking Away the Ladder*	解析张夏准《富国陷阱：发达国家为何踢开梯子》	经济学
An Analysis of Thomas Robert Malthus's *An Essay on the Principle of Population*	解析托马斯·罗伯特·马尔萨斯《人口论》	经济学

An Analysis of John Maynard Keynes's *The General Theory of Employment, Interest and Money*	解析约翰·梅纳德·凯恩斯《就业、利息和货币通论》	经济学
An Analysis of Milton Friedman's *The Role of Monetary Policy*	解析米尔顿·弗里德曼《货币政策的作用》	经济学
An Analysis of Burton G. Malkiel's *A Random Walk Down Wall Street*	解析伯顿·G. 马尔基尔《漫步华尔街》	经济学
An Analysis of Friedrich A. Hayek's *The Road to Serfdom*	解析弗里德里希·A. 哈耶克《通往奴役之路》	经济学
An Analysis of Charles P. Kindleberger's *Manias, Panics, and Crashes: A History of Financial Crises*	解析查尔斯·P. 金德尔伯格《疯狂、惊恐和崩溃：金融危机史》	经济学
An Analysis of Amartya Sen's *Development as Freedom*	解析阿马蒂亚·森《以自由看待发展》	经济学
An Analysis of Rachel Carson's *Silent Spring*	解析蕾切尔·卡森《寂静的春天》	地理学
An Analysis of Charles Darwin's *On the Origin of Species: by Means of Natural Selection, or The Preservation of Favoured Races in the Struggle for Life*	解析查尔斯·达尔文《物种起源》	地理学
An Analysis of World Commission on Environment and Development's *The Brundtland Report, Our Common Future*	解析世界环境与发展委员会《布伦特兰报告：我们共同的未来》	地理学
An Analysis of James E. Lovelock's *Gaia: A New Look at Life on Earth*	解析詹姆斯·E. 拉伍洛克《盖娅：地球生命的新视野》	地理学
An Analysis of Paul Kennedy's *The Rise and Fall of the Great Powers: Economic Change and Military Conflict from 1500—2000*	解析保罗·肯尼迪《大国的兴衰：1500—2000 年的经济变革与军事冲突》	历史
An Analysis of Janet L. Abu-Lughod's *Before European Hegemony: The World System A. D. 1250—1350*	解析珍妮特·L. 阿布-卢格霍德《欧洲霸权之前：1250—1350 年的世界体系》	历史
An Analysis of Alfred W. Crosby's *The Columbian Exchange: Biological and Cultural Consequences of 1492*	解析艾尔弗雷德·W. 克罗斯比《哥伦布大交换：1492 年以后的生物影响和文化冲击》	历史
An Analysis of Tony Judt's *Postwar: A History of Europe since 1945*	解析托尼·朱特《战后欧洲史》	历史
An Analysis of Richard J. Evans's *In Defence of History*	解析理查德·J. 艾文斯《捍卫历史》	历史
An Analysis of Eric Hobsbawm's *The Age of Revolution: Europe 1789–1848*	解析艾瑞克·霍布斯鲍姆《革命的年代：欧洲 1789—1848 年》	历史

An Analysis of Roland Barthes's *Mythologies*	解析罗兰·巴特《神话学》	文学与批判理论
An Analysis of Simone de Beauvoir's *The Second Sex*	解析西蒙娜·德·波伏娃《第二性》	文学与批判理论
An Analysis of Edward W. Said's *Orientalism*	解析爱德华·W. 萨义德《东方主义》	文学与批判理论
An Analysis of Virginia Woolf's *A Room of One's Own*	解析弗吉尼亚·伍尔芙《一间自己的房间》	文学与批判理论
An Analysis of Judith Butler's *Gender Trouble*	解析朱迪斯·巴特勒《性别麻烦》	文学与批判理论
An Analysis of Ferdinand de Saussure's *Course in General Linguistics*	解析费尔迪南·德·索绪尔《普通语言学教程》	文学与批判理论
An Analysis of Susan Sontag's *On Photography*	解析苏珊·桑塔格《论摄影》	文学与批判理论
An Analysis of Walter Benjamin's *The Work of Art in the Age of Mechanical Reproduction*	解析瓦尔特·本雅明《机械复制时代的艺术作品》	文学与批判理论
An Analysis of W.E.B. Du Bois's *The Souls of Black Folk*	解析 W.E.B. 杜波依斯《黑人的灵魂》	文学与批判理论
An Analysis of Plato's *The Republic*	解析柏拉图《理想国》	哲学
An Analysis of Plato's *Symposium*	解析柏拉图《会饮篇》	哲学
An Analysis of Aristotle's *Metaphysics*	解析亚里士多德《形而上学》	哲学
An Analysis of Aristotle's *Nicomachean Ethics*	解析亚里士多德《尼各马可伦理学》	哲学
An Analysis of Immanuel Kant's *Critique of Pure Reason*	解析伊曼努尔·康德《纯粹理性批判》	哲学
An Analysis of Ludwig Wittgenstein's *Philosophical Investigations*	解析路德维希·维特根斯坦《哲学研究》	哲学
An Analysis of G.W.F. Hegel's *Phenomenology of Spirit*	解析 G.W.F. 黑格尔《精神现象学》	哲学
An Analysis of Baruch Spinoza's *Ethics*	解析巴鲁赫·斯宾诺莎《伦理学》	哲学
An Analysis of Hannah Arendt's *The Human Condition*	解析汉娜·阿伦特《人的境况》	哲学
An Analysis of G.E.M. Anscombe's *Modern Moral Philosophy*	解析 G.E.M. 安斯康姆《现代道德哲学》	哲学
An Analysis of David Hume's *An Enquiry Concerning Human Understanding*	解析大卫·休谟《人类理解研究》	哲学

An Analysis of Søren Kierkegaard's *Fear and Trembling*	解析索伦·克尔凯郭尔《恐惧与战栗》	哲学
An Analysis of René Descartes's *Meditations on First Philosophy*	解析勒内·笛卡尔《第一哲学沉思录》	哲学
An Analysis of Friedrich Nietzsche's *On the Genealogy of Morality*	解析弗里德里希·尼采《论道德的谱系》	哲学
An Analysis of Gilbert Ryle's *The Concept of Mind*	解析吉尔伯特·赖尔《心的概念》	哲学
An Analysis of Thomas Kuhn's *The Structure of Scientific Revolutions*	解析托马斯·库恩《科学革命的结构》	哲学
An Analysis of John Stuart Mill's *Utilitarianism*	解析约翰·斯图亚特·穆勒《功利主义》	哲学
An Analysis of Aristotle's *Politics*	解析亚里士多德《政治学》	政治学
An Analysis of Niccolò Machiavelli's *The Prince*	解析尼科洛·马基雅利《君主论》	政治学
An Analysis of Karl Marx's *Capital*	解析卡尔·马克思《资本论》	政治学
An Analysis of Benedict Anderson's *Imagined Communities*	解析本尼迪克特·安德森《想象的共同体》	政治学
An Analysis of Samuel P. Huntington's *The Clash of Civilizations and the Remaking of World Order*	解析塞缪尔·P.亨廷顿《文明的冲突与世界秩序的重建》	政治学
An Analysis of Alexis de Tocqueville's *Democracy in America*	解析阿列克西·德·托克维尔《论美国的民主》	政治学
An Analysis of John A. Hobson's *Imperialism: A Study*	解析约翰·A.霍布森《帝国主义》	政治学
An Analysis of Thomas Paine's *Common Sense*	解析托马斯·潘恩《常识》	政治学
An Analysis of John Rawls's *A Theory of Justice*	解析约翰·罗尔斯《正义论》	政治学
An Analysis of Francis Fukuyama's *The End of History and the Last Man*	解析弗朗西斯·福山《历史的终结与最后的人》	政治学
An Analysis of John Locke's *Two Treatises of Government*	解析约翰·洛克《政府论》	政治学
An Analysis of Sun Tzu's *The Art of War*	解析孙武《孙子兵法》	政治学
An Analysis of Henry Kissinger's *World Order: Reflections on the Character of Nations and the Course of History*	解析亨利·基辛格《世界秩序》	政治学
An Analysis of Jean-Jacques Rousseau's *The Social Contract*	解析让-雅克·卢梭《社会契约论》	政治学

An Analysis of Odd Arne Westad's *The Global Cold War: Third World Interventions and the Making of Our Times*	解析文安立《全球冷战：美苏对第三世界的干涉与当代世界的形成》	政治学
An Analysis of Sigmund Freud's *The Interpretation of Dreams*	解析西格蒙德·弗洛伊德《梦的解析》	心理学
An Analysis of William James' *The Principles of Psychology*	解析威廉·詹姆斯《心理学原理》	心理学
An Analysis of Philip Zimbardo's *The Lucifer Effect*	解析菲利普·津巴多《路西法效应》	心理学
An Analysis of Leon Festinger's *A Theory of Cognitive Dissonance*	解析利昂·费斯汀格《认知失调论》	心理学
An Analysis of Richard H. Thaler & Cass R. Sunstein's *Nudge: Improving Decisions about Health, Wealth, and Happiness*	解析理查德·H.泰勒/卡斯·R.桑斯坦《助推：如何做出有关健康、财富和幸福的更优决策》	心理学
An Analysis of Gordon Allport's *The Nature of Prejudice*	解析高尔登·奥尔波特《偏见的本质》	心理学
An Analysis of Steven Pinker's *The Better Angels of Our Nature: Why Violence Has Declined*	解析斯蒂芬·平克《人性中的善良天使：暴力为什么会减少》	心理学
An Analysis of Stanley Milgram's *Obedience to Authority*	解析斯坦利·米尔格拉姆《对权威的服从》	心理学
An Analysis of Betty Friedan's *The Feminine Mystique*	解析贝蒂·弗里丹《女性的奥秘》	心理学
An Analysis of David Riesman's *The Lonely Crowd: A Study of the Changing American Character*	解析大卫·理斯曼《孤独的人群：美国人社会性格演变之研究》	社会学
An Analysis of Franz Boas's *Race, Language and Culture*	解析弗朗兹·博厄斯《种族、语言与文化》	社会学
An Analysis of Pierre Bourdieu's *Outline of a Theory of Practice*	解析皮埃尔·布尔迪厄《实践理论大纲》	社会学
An Analysis of Max Weber's *The Protestant Ethic and the Spirit of Capitalism*	解析马克斯·韦伯《新教伦理与资本主义精神》	社会学
An Analysis of Jane Jacobs's *The Death and Life of Great American Cities*	解析简·雅各布斯《美国大城市的死与生》	社会学
An Analysis of C. Wright Mills's *The Sociological Imagination*	解析C.赖特·米尔斯《社会学的想象力》	社会学
An Analysis of Robert E. Lucas Jr.'s *Why Doesn't Capital Flow from Rich to Poor Countries?*	解析小罗伯特·E.卢卡斯《为何资本不从富国流向穷国？》	社会学

An Analysis of Émile Durkheim's *On Suicide*	解析埃米尔·迪尔凯姆《自杀论》	社会学
An Analysis of Eric Hoffer's *The True Believer: Thoughts on the Nature of Mass Movements*	解析埃里克·霍弗《狂热分子：群众运动圣经》	社会学
An Analysis of Jared M. Diamond's *Collapse: How Societies Choose to Fail or Survive*	解析贾雷德·M.戴蒙德《大崩溃：社会如何选择兴亡》	社会学
An Analysis of Michel Foucault's *The History of Sexuality Vol. 1: The Will to Knowledge*	解析米歇尔·福柯《性史（第一卷）：求知意志》	社会学
An Analysis of Michel Foucault's *Discipline and Punish*	解析米歇尔·福柯《规训与惩罚》	社会学
An Analysis of Richard Dawkins's *The Selfish Gene*	解析理查德·道金斯《自私的基因》	社会学
An Analysis of Antonio Gramsci's *Prison Notebooks*	解析安东尼奥·葛兰西《狱中札记》	社会学
An Analysis of Augustine's *Confessions*	解析奥古斯丁《忏悔录》	神学
An Analysis of C. S. Lewis's *The Abolition of Man*	解析 C. S. 路易斯《人之废》	神学

图书在版编目（CIP）数据

解析W. E. B.杜波伊斯《黑人的灵魂》/ 詹森·克西迪亚斯（Jason Xidias）著；王作伟译. —上海：上海外语教育出版社，2020
（世界思想宝库钥匙丛书）
ISBN 978-7-5446-6118-8

Ⅰ.①解… Ⅱ.①詹… ②王… Ⅲ.①杜波伊斯（DuBois, William Edward Burghardt 1868-1963）—文学研究 Ⅳ.①I712.065

中国版本图书馆CIP数据核字（2020）第014463号

This Chinese-English bilingual edition of *An Analysis of W. E. B. Du Bois's* The Souls of Black Folk is published by arrangement with Macat International Limited.
Licensed for sale throughout the world.

本书汉英双语版由Macat国际有限公司授权上海外语教育出版社有限公司出版。
供在全世界范围内发行、销售。

图字：09 – 2018 – 549

出版发行：上海外语教育出版社
　　　　　（上海外国语大学内）　邮编：200083
电　　话：021-65425300（总机）
电子邮箱：bookinfo@sflep.com.cn
网　　址：http://www.sflep.com
责任编辑：梁瀚杰

印　　刷：上海华教印务有限公司
开　　本：890×1240　1/32　印张 5.625　字数 115千字
版　　次：2020 年 5月第 1版　2020 年 5月第 1次印刷
印　　数：2 100 册

书　　号：ISBN 978-7-5446-6118-8
定　　价：30.00 元
　　　本版图书如有印装质量问题，可向本社调换
　　　质量服务热线：4008-213-263　电子邮箱：editorial@sflep.com